A World of Adventure Discovery and Dreams

Published by Book Hub Publishing

For further information re national & international distribution:
www.bookhubpublishing.com
 info@bookhubpublishing.com
@BookHubPublish

Printed in the Republic of Ireland

First Edition 2018

ISBN 978-1-9998951-9-8

A catalogue record for this book is available from the British Library.

This publication is sold with the understanding that the Publisher/Author is not engaged in rendering health, legal services or other professional services. If legal advice, health or other expert assistance is required, the services of a competent, qualified professional person should be sought.

INTRODUCTION

Welcome to the world of adventure discovery and dreams at home and on adventure abroad. Among tree plants and posies, bees, butterflies and bunny rabbits, at one with nature in contrasting natural environments.

Stories of friends, adventures, discovery and dreams from the woodlands and meadows to a world of high-powered deal making. With a king in his castle, and evil warriors in unknown lands to narrow escapes in a tropical rain forest, a race through a vineyard, encounters with a robot and a stranded sleigh ride with huskies in the snow.

Stories of friends and adventures their discoveries and dreams, with some yet to come true.

Warmest wishes for inspiration, celebration, joy and peace, across visible and invisible borders, from my world to yours, wherever you may be.

Ann

*It seems to me that the natural world
is the greatest source of excitement;
The greatest source of visual beauty;
The greatest source of intellectual interest;
The greatest source of so much in life,
that makes life worth living"*

By Sir David Attenborough, in interview with the BBC 2006

DEDICATION

I dedicate this book to all those wonderful, kind and inspirational folks nearby and far away, who in so many instances, have shaped and influence my world positively, through words and actions, I wish you a life of endless joy and celebration.

To all those who have stepped in to help, care for and support, or stepped back, so as not to hurt or hinder others on life's path, I wish you a lifetime of magic moments.

To my nearest and dearest now departed, I wish you peace and everlasting love.

To everyone on our shared planet who enjoys the beauty of nature and contrasting environments and to all those **who** endeavour to protect, secure and enhance planet Earth for future generations, I give you A World of Adventure, Discovery and Dreams, and hope yours all come true.

Welcome to A World of Adventure, Discovery and Dreams in contrasting environments. From the meadows, and woodlands to imaginary sci-fi, futuristic planets and the disruptive powers of an ever changing technological world, where the beauty of nature and the natural environment is a constant and permanent force, despite the adverse impact of climate change.

Story focus: Nature and contrasting environments and Climate Change. Ideas are presented on SMART, futuristic environments and Robotics.

KEY THEMES REFERENCED IN STORY SERIES:

Nature and contrasting natural environments referenced in urban, rural, island and inland settings, with reference to events in meadows, mountains, lakes, rivers, oceans and forests.

Technological development and futuristic imaginary environments referenced in chapter on robots, the imaginary dark planet and more current developments in futuristic and space age environments, as played out at the movies.

Climate Change and its impact on the natural and business environments globally.

TABLE OF CONTENTS

Chapters 1 - 7 will appeal to junior readers (age range 9/10yrs)

Chapters 8 - 16 will appeal to the more advanced reader (age range 11/13yrs)

1

MEET THE FRIENDS

Meet Bow, Buddy, and Perry the poodle, three puppies that are best friends. The three friends play together, stay together and compete for attention and treats.

Bow is brown and white, the lazy puppy who enjoys short bursts of activity with Perry and Buddy and other friends close by.

Buddy is ginger and white, the energetic and adventurous puppy who likes to play and explore in the meadow and woodlands.

Perry the poodle is completely snow white, the timid and impulsive one, who is happy to follow closely and cautiously along until something of interest catches his eye.

Buddy, Bow and Perry are surrounded by friendly and unfriendly neighbours who live close by and in the meadows and woodlands.

There is a lake with a magic mountain in the distance. Folk's fish, sail, picnic and pony trek around the lake in sunny weather.

The school is a short walk from the village green and on occasion, boys and girls stop by to visit the three friends, sometimes sharing leftover lunch snacks or sweet treats.

The town is further away by the river. The ocean is close by and the islands beyond are a short boat trip from the harbour.

The three friends enjoy their routine walks and runs through the woodlands and meadows, a wrestle with Felix the cat, and from time to time the occasional trip to town, or movie moments with strange folk from other planets. So there is always something of interest to amuse, annoy, surprise, or scare the friends, with stories of adventures, discovery and dreams at home and abroad.

2

NEIGHBOURS AND FRIENDS

Buddy, Bow, and Perry the poodle are surrounded by lots of friends and neighbours. Who live in the nearby woodland, pastureland and meadow and visit from time to time. Some are friendly and others are very unfriendly, like the speedy rabbit with his ever increasing family and friends, the fox and hare families, Felix the cat, Hunter and Polly the ponies, and various members of the birds, bees and duck families.

On occasion, Felix the cat joins the friends at play, before escaping over the wall quickly with a loud meow when overwhelmed from wrestling with the three friends, as they are so much stronger. At such times, Felix uses all his strength and sharp claws to escape beyond their reach.

Polly the pony, Cooper the baby foal and Hunter the horse live in the meadow in summer. There is an orchard on one side and juicy apples fall over the wall into the meadow in the autumn. Polly and Cooper enjoy a munch of the delicious red and yellow apples.

Sometimes they gallop through the field as if showing off, and return to the garden wall to see if Buddy, Perry the Poodle, Bow or the other friends noticed.

The ponies love summer as the weather is warm and they go on longer treks around the countryside, down narrow lanes and bushy roads through the village by the lake, and onwards to the paddock to perfect their jumping skills.

Winter is the dullest and harshest season for the ponies. Even with warm winter covers, they are still cold especially when the freezing north wind blows, oftentimes-bringing snow and ice. It is also dark by early evening, so Hunter, Polly, and Cooper the foal must remain indoors for a longer time and wait for Farmer Ted to feed them.

Soon it will be spring again, the days will be longer, the weather warmer, and Polly and Hunter will be back in their favourite home, the meadow. They will also lose their woolly winter covers and go trekking again.

3

ADVENTURES IN THE
COUNTRYSIDE AND BEYOND

Mrs Mallery lives down a long winding path through the woods that lead to her Cottage. The children said the front door of the old cottage is like a chocolate bar and the thatched cottage roof like honeycomb. The children think it's a magical place and love going for walks there.

The path is tree-lined all the way to the cottage door. There are the large oak trees, clusters of hazel, blackthorn, hawthorn, willow, sycamore, elder and ash trees all dotted around. These deciduous trees provide shelter against the harsh winter winds and a cool shade from the warm summer sun. Many beautiful plants, flowers and berries also grow in abundance, especially during the spring, summer and autumn seasons.

There is also an upside-down tree, where the children occasionally stop to play and hide under when in the woods.

Mrs Mallery has a walled vegetable and herb garden and an orchard where the sweetest most delicious apples, blackberries, gooseberries, blackcurrants and plums grow.

Through the gate at the side of the cottage is a stream and on the other side of the stream towards the woods is a tree house, that fascinates the children and they all love to play there.

Mrs Mallery has ducks, hens and seven adorable chicks that she now keeps in the grassy area off the orchard. There were eight, but the fox came one lunchtime and took one when all were grazing and swimming with the ducks in the stream. Last time one chick went missing just before it was time to put them into the barn for the evening.

Hatty the hen was all flustered and Mrs Mallery at first didn't know why. Then she noticed the missing chick and panicked as she thought the fox had been back again.

She then saw Hatty and her chicks all chirping going towards the tree house by the stream. Hatty pushed her way through the little gate and in the small door of the tree house. As soon as the door opened, out popped the little lost chick followed closely by a forlorn frog that leaped in the direction of the nearby stream.

Buddy went to the tree house one time for his own sniff inside. What a strange place thought Buddy as he looked around. The first level was circular with seating around the edge and an oval table in the centre.

On the table was a tea set; with the tiniest cups and saucers, he had ever seen. Leading on to the next level was a tall ladder with large square steps.

Buddy could only climb two of the eight steps, just high enough to see through the door to the small window at the top.

Mrs Mallery said all the children loved to play in the tree house and she then recounted stories to Adrianna about how some children from junior school once came on a summer camping break and thought the tree house was haunted.

As they saw a light through the window in the distance and at the top was a large white and dark shape swaying back and forth in the night breeze.

The children were fascinated and some jokily suggested that maybe the fairies had come to play; the sighting spooked others, who were certain at least from the distance and in the reflection of moonlight, the tree house was haunted.

As mystery and intrigue grew at the possibility of ghosts or 'other world' creatures at play in the tree house, Mr Breen their teacher had to quiet their suspicions by going there one evening to explore.

On another occasion, boys and girls came on a school visit to the woodlands to gather flowers, paint and draw. Susie, one of the little girls slipped away through the leafy path that leads to the tree house and went inside to explore. She climbed up the steps to the next level.

When suddenly the old rusty latch fell on the tree house door, then the latch jammed and Susie was unable to open the door.

Susie tried again to lift the old rusty latch, but couldn't and started to cry calling out in a whimpering little voice – "help, help, I am locked in the tree house, help, please somebody help me!!"

At the same time, the teacher Mrs Condry who was giving an art demonstration to the boys and girls on colours of nature, noticed Susie was missing, stopped and called out, "Susie, Susie, where are you"... but no reply. "Ok boys and girls, gather up your belongings quickly, and follow me, we must find Susie," said a panicked Mrs Condry.

So the children followed Mrs Condry, calling out "Susie, Susie" where are you", as they continued down the long winding path through the woods.

When they got closer to the tree house, they heard sobbing cries for help. The children immediately shouted out, "Susie, Susie we are here." "I am in the tree house," said Susie.

"It's ok now Susie, we are here, why don't you come down from the tree house? I will help you," said Mrs Condry. "The latch is stuck and I cannot open the door," replied Susie, sobbing.

"Oh dear let's see," said Mrs Condry, as she peered up at the tree house while the boys and girls silently looked on. "Darling keep calm and be brave, we will find a way to help you down very shortly," but Susie continued sobbing.

Next thing, farmer Fred appeared and greeted all. "Is everything ok? I heard all the talk from the field across the river," said Farmer Fred.

"Fred, good to see you, Susie is stuck at the top of the tree house, the door latch jammed, so we need something to wench open the door, a ladder would also be useful," said Mrs Condry.

Farmer Fred went across to Mrs Mallery's cottage and got a tall ladder and mallet. He then climbed up to the small window and passed Susie the mallet, and instructed the sobbing and scared Susie to be brave and strong and try to push the mallet under the latch.

Susie followed Farmer Fred's instructions using all her strength; pressed the mallet under the latch, leaning with all her weight until the latch finally snapped and fell onto the floor and the door swung open.

All the children cheered and clapped – "she's done it, the door is open."
"I am coming down," said Susie.

Mrs Condry and all the children rushed over to Susie, some children clapped hands, and others gave Susie a big hug. "We're so delighted you're safe and well Susie, everyone was very worried about you," said a relieved Mrs Condry.

"What on earth made you come here in the first place without telling anyone? Did someone upset you or was something worrying you," asked Mrs Condry.

"My older sister Cara and her friends took my dolly along to play in the tree house that time, and forgot to bring her back home.

I missed my dolly terribly and had a dream about how the fairies were going to give her away to evil warriors in exchange for a princess, like the story I read and movie I saw at Easter," explained Susie.

"Really, that sounds scary, tell us what happened," said Mrs Condry. All the children then gathered around on the grass to listen as Susie recounted her dream. "In my dream, I imagined my dolly having a fantastic happy and fun time among woodland friends and fairies." All alone under the smiling eyes of the Moon and when she went to sleep, a million more bright stars sparkled in the night sky lighting up the woodland world for all the fairies, leprechauns and creatures of the night as they came out to play and party.

Then they had a grand party and the fairies put a beautiful gown on my dolly and made her a goddess of darkness. They even gave her magic powers to dispel evil during the night. The Fairies placed her high in the trees from where she could see everyone and everything in the forest during party celebrations. Others climbed up to help her keep watch too. While the fairies and leprechauns danced, and sang merrily below as the stars sparkled brightly in the night sky above.

It all seemed like a magical world, as the music, song, and party celebrations continued, other forest friends also appeared. The badgers emerged from his sett deep in the undergrowth to gather food for winter hibernation, just like the hedgehog who appeared, also searching for food and a place to hibernate. The fox went by as he hunted for food to feed his little cubs in their den. A couple of bunny rabbits emerged from their warren and played close to the rocks by the stream.

The only other disruption to the party celebrations was the scary long-eared bats just like the type I saw in the movie that flew back and forth as if wanting to join the fun, but were too busy hunting for food before going into hibernation. And the cooing owls who reminded everyone it was getting very late for party fun and frolics as they stood watch with their big eyes gleaming from the tall oak and sycamore trees. The fairies knew then they must disappear before dawn leaving my dolly all alone.

Then the Snow Queen flew by in her sparkling silver frosted coach, which was drawn by four snow white horses that came to an instant stop close to the big tree, on seeing the elder fairy Jabokie. She was very distressed and looking for help to rescue her princess from evil invaders who attacked from another universe while searching for lost treasure. She was telling the elder fairy, Jabokie how evil warriors came in the night looking for lost treasures that fell to earth on their last voyage. Others gathered round as the Snow Queen recounted how evil invaders stole her princess and will not release her until she gives them the treasure, recovered by fishermen in their nets when deep ocean fishing. She then went on to recount details the full salvage operation.

The Snow Queen then explained how they sent large vessels from her shipping fleet to assist in the recovery mission. But insisted this was the treasure from her great grandfather's expeditions to foreign lands. On their return they got caught in high seas and lost almost all the cargo including a sizable amount of gold and other precious metals, ceramic jars, spices, rich fabrics, and liquor along with their voyage documentation and treasure maps. Many items were luckily salvaged and the cargo was mostly intact which is surprising, as it's more than two hundred years old.

"The ocean was clear blue on the surface but further down in the deep it was another colourful magical world, with a diverse landscape. There are expanses of sandy desert, areas of stony and rocky seabed surfaces, cliffs, caves and mountains.

In fact, the world's longest mountain range is found underwater along with deep crevice and rocky inlets that are home to a multitude of fish, flora and fauna, including various sea mosses, animal and plant anemone, crustaceans, green, brown and red algae, coral reefs, sponge, plankton and kelp," explained the Snow Queen.

"We sent the otters to explore and assist my team initially," said the snow Queen. As according to our special forces, the sea otters were capable and cleaver, using rocks and other available material as tools, to assist their survival and salvage efforts on this mission. The sea otters were one of the few mammals with the ability to use tools which proved useful on this mission to salvage what remained of the sunken cargo," said the Snow Queen.

"The sea otters are also credited with protecting the kelp forests from destruction by feeding on the sea urchins in their warmer native waters. Thus reducing their numbers and power to damage the kelp forests and we thought they would be useful on this mission in removing the build up of various sea algae and dislodging rocks and unwanted debris from in and around the sunken cargo.

There were millions of multi-coloured fish and larger predatory folk, like the various members of the shark family who moved quickly and preferred the open waters of the ocean, unless food was scarce there.

Ocean mammals like the dolphins were friendly and inquisitive as they passed by even showing off from time to time as they leaped above the water; the blue whales with their young were noticeable and distinct from the other twenty-four whale species that visit our shore, by their enormous size and presence.
The other ocean inhabitants kept out of their way as the whales dominated the water but luckily totally ignored activity around the sunken cargo.

Less obvious creatures emerged closer to the rocks where the cargo ran aground before sinking. Some starfish, an octopus, limpets, scallops, muscles, lobsters were visible in and around the rocks. Various members of the crab family, like the tiny hermit crab and velvet crab in deeper water of the rocky inlet, were also visible.

Other fish varieties like the greater piper fish, rock goby and blennies emerged from time to time among the seaweed in the rocky pool.

"The glistening green-blue surface of the ocean hid tales of sunken treasures from centuries old voyages of discovery or military battles at sea, buried among the flora and fauna, that is home to the many schools and shoals of fish, large and small who inhabited the deep blue ocean," sighed the Snow Queen.

Our otters were amazed by the small multi-coloured fish in these cooler waters, all swimming much too fast to count, catch for dinner or even identify. This left the otters momentarily deflated – but not defeated, as they did catch a glimpse of some wrasse, pollack and gobies swimming over the rocks among the kelp.

Colourful animal and plant anemone like the jewelled and the snakelock anemone, dead-mans-fingers, and some globular urchins that lived in the kelp forests, were visible especially during hours of bright sunlight or on moonlit nights, even though the waters around the sunken treasure were dark.

Some fish species changed colour as a camouflage for protection and were less visible, for example, the flat fish, are white on top and speckled brown underneath, Place are similar but have orange spots. The Lesser sand eels were green and black, and then silver and white underneath. The Exotic long spined scorpions and sand goby all changed colour to blend in, or were a similar colour to their environment.

Others hid like the lesser weaver fish who buries itself in the sand on the lower shore, with just eyes showing, this fish can also inflict a painful sting if stood on, according to the otters.

Members of the shellfish family like limpets, barnacles and muscles lived on more exposed rocky seashore areas -hidden among the brown seaweed, pink coralline algae and colourful sea anemone of these unfamiliar cooler waters.

The otters were pleased that their favourite sea urchins and surprisingly large plant anemone were in abundance along with a variety of shellfish to provide a tasty meal.

But the otters didn't like this cooler ocean, even though their mission was interesting and provided the opportunity to explore the shoreline with its long stony beach, sand dunes and salt marshes to the towering cliffs beyond, with a snow white castle lighthouse visible on the horizon.

They preferred the intertidal zone, which is between low and high tide. This intertidal environment is made up of, an upper, a middle and lower shore, where animal and plant life is extremely varied, depending on whether the shore area was muddy, rocky or sandy.

The salvage location in the Estuary was tricky, for starters, the water was muddy and cooler, the goggles were uncomfortable, the unexpected ocean currents were scary especially when very strong.

Oftentimes washing the otters onto the rocks to the alarm of the native seabirds, like the guillemot gulls and sandpipers, who would call out in a panicked loud shrill at the sudden interruption to their world. Other shoreline inhabitants, like the seals, limpets, muscles, butterfly fish and ling, looked up from under the rocks, startled by the sudden arrival of the otters, who were crushed, bruised and in pain on the rocks, among indifferent and unwelcoming friends.

The seals mumbled among themselves as they lazed around on the shore, while staying close to their young who were rolling in the regular bladderwrack seaweed, and other seashore vegetation, like red foliose algae, pink coralline algae and thong weeds that covered part of the rocks. However, the seals were fast swimmers underwater as they hunted for prey to feed their young, from the selection of available fish, totally ignoring the salvage operation and the challenges faced by the sea otters in these cooler waters.

And they couldn't count on the native otters for guidance or assistance either, as they mostly inhabited inland lakes and rivers, avoiding salt water as it damaged their fur, venturing out of their holt at dusk to hunt for food, which was mainly fish, waterfowl and frogs.

Still, the otters managed to enjoy their favourite feast of snails and worms from the many varieties found in abundance on the rocky, sandy and muddy seashore areas. Their favourite honey-comb worms, green leaf worms and sand-hoppers were available on the sandy and rocky shore area along with some black, green and potato heart sea urchins. The otters also liked to feast on the rag worm, lugworms and heart anemone that lived burrowed in the muddy sandy seashore, but often competed for such juicy worm offerings with the smaller migratory birds like the sanderlings, dunlins, turnstones, and lapwing.

The common seagulls made such an unnecessary racket, even tried one time to peck Harvey and his two friends, as they recovered from a strong current that hurled them ashore on a flat muddy area of the shore. That is also a fertile feeding ground for the sea birds, and migratory geese from the Brent and Barnacle families, who graze on the sea grasses of the surrounding mudflats.

The razorbills and guillemots members of the gull family created a noisy chorus overhead that made everyone nervous, as they fished for food and competed for attention with the black back gulls, the smaller delicate kittiwakes, the large herring gulls and the visiting terns, skuas and petrels.

The puffins and gannets remained silent and observed from the craggy nearby cliffs while keeping a careful watch over their young. A couple of ravens circled searching for prey, as did a golden eagle.
The previous week a much stronger ocean current swept the otters out into the deep blue ocean. Leaving them shivering, choking and frantically swimming under and over water to avoid detection from dangerous predators, to reach their search and exploration position by the lost cargo.

The most exciting part of the underwater discovery mission was locating the sunken vessel, after the fishermen recovered some cargo in their fishing nets that time.

The most difficult part of the salvage operation was firstly locating the cargo on the vessel and in the surrounding waters and then bringing it to the surface.

There were large chests in a decaying delicate state, lying among the coral and sea algae and muddy dark water to contend with, as they tried to move what remained of the cargo from the sunken vessel.

The most fascinating part of all according to our special forces sent to explore the area with the otters was discovering emeralds and gold treasure in almost perfect condition in a small metal chest. The metal and porcelain artefact survived too along with a couple of sealed wooden containers, but they were in a very fragile condition.

They also found the anchor, a telescope in near perfect condition, a compass with a Chinese inscription, a large bunch of keys, an inkwell, a document seal, glass crystal pitchers containing liquor and some ceramic clay jars.

The Snow Queen thought it ironic that the rocks that caused the ship to sink in stormy weather, now provided a secure, stable and sheltered underwater location that helped to preserve the cargo from the rough currents of open seas.

"Unfortunately, we still have not been able to bring the vessel to the surface due to its size, weight, and creaking, decaying, delicate state. Even though the mask and part of the bow were in good condition, the hull was less stable and more difficult to reach," explained the Snow Queen.

Special equipment was then used to take the cargo to the surface and onward to my palace to store securely. "That's the only treasure we know about Jabokie and I will not part with such a precious part of history, regardless who sets claim to it. We also had to work by night, but noticed nothing suspicious when recovering or transporting the cargo of old treasure.

"Unless something in the cargo caught the evil warriors signal as they searched our planet. Metal, diamonds, or crystal may have triggered a remote signal," said Jabokie.

"As we discovered on our mission to the Dark plant to recover black diamond's evil invaders stole from the Emperors. The black diamonds were used to signal earth in an effort to locate and access specific target areas," said Jabokie. "But we never saw anything unusual or felt we were being observed by such evil warriors – why would they be concerned; I was just reclaiming what was mine and didn't wish to harm or hurt anyone," explained the anxious Snow Queen.

"Oh my God, actually there was something," said the Snow Queen, "but I'm sure it's of little use." "Please Precious One do tell me, it could matter very much" said Jabokie. Viber his senior officer was suddenly very alert and moved closer. "Well just one evening towards the end of the recovery mission, there was some talk among the special forces, joking that the old sunken ship was haunted, as a blinding sparkling light surrounded the ship for a couple of minutes, then disappeared. Only to return with short bursts of blinding light lasting a couple of seconds that darted around the ship and then disappeared again - but perhaps it was the rays of the setting sun or moon rising," said the Snow Queen.

"I fear they want your diamonds or they think you have something they lost along the way," said Jabokie. "Either way we have a problem Precious One, so the sooner we start to solve the problem, the quicker your princess will be rescued and safely back home to her castle in the snow..

"So do not fret, Precious One, we will do everything possible to help you," said Jabokie to the very anxious Snow Queen

"I know I can depend on you Jabokie, you and your people are much cleverer, move faster, and senior officers tell me you never fail on any mission," said a hopeful sounding Snow Queen.

"Ah you probably heard of our various mission and the one I mentioned to the Dark Planet to recover the diamonds for the Emperor," replied Jabokie.

"It was such a dangerous mission as we were confronted by Robot warriors and tall Alien folk," said Jabokie, who then continued to recount details of their various missions to the Snow Queen as she tried to steady her horses at the same time. "Don't forget, this is a top secret mission," said the Snow Queen. "Oh Precious One, all our missions are a top-secret, as they are all extremely difficult and dangerous, usually into strange lands or unfamiliar planets.

And I expect this operation to free your princess will be just as difficult, Precious One, especially if we discover she is on the Dark planet," said Jabokie.

"During our first and second undercover investigation mission to the Dark planet the week before, we could see whole communities of similar type robots busily working as if building a huge ship or aircraft. Their work was being examined by a group of tall alien figures with spikes from their head. It was so weird. We decided nothing on the Dark planet was humanlike in any way and were nervous," said Jabokie.

"But our mission was to recover the Emperors precious diamonds, that on further investigation we discovered were about to be used for signalling Earth and communicating with other planets before launching an invasion.

The black diamond's were also the Emperors prized possession, and had been in his family for almost a thousand years. They had increased in value with each passing year and no doubt had special powers, or so the evil invaders on the Dark planet seemed to think. So, our challenge was firstly to locate the diamonds on this highly patrolled and organised planet, recover and return them safely to the Emperor," said Jabokie.

"It took two initial discovery missions, before we found the vault where the diamonds were stored. Which was in a high security area close to where the robots and other alien-looking folk were working on the large tank or plane?

Even the flowers and plants on the Dark planet seemed to serve an electronic function, lighting up ground as folk went by and changing colours, so next time you looked, the yellow flowers were blue. Further along in what resembled tall trees were a couple of smaller birds with laser- lights beaming from their eyes that lit up the ground around the entrance the warehouse and vault.

The trucks and jeeps even drove themselves and when they stopped close to the huge workshop, doors opened automatically and an arm like structure took the load from the trucks and placed it inside the warehouse or sometimes in a huge vault outside the high wall.

Along the way different groups of people seemed to exist in huge enclosures where young and old lived together like in the noble families of Italy centuries ago. Some were playing board games, others sitting in rows looking at a huge chart and making notes.

Further back, there were robot's in action mode, some swirling around, others jumping as if practicing their various moves. They were able to power into the air and land at a specific point with aliens checking their landing position and making notes. Those robots who failed to land at the correct point had to repeat the act. Several more followed, but on landing, changed shape to fit through a narrow space between two beams.

A group of junior robots arrived in what looked like a glass train. They went to an activity area to practice a range of activities like climbing, sliding, balancing, long jumps and were coached by both robots and aliens for about two hours.

Everything inside and outside the huge wall appeared to be electronic with any irregularity leading to loud bleeping sounds, followed by instructions over their public-address system to "neutralise alarm at point C or deactivate alarm in area B.

There were large electronic insects resembling spiders connecting strands across the large tank-like machine the robots were working on. And two huge birds placing twigs on the upper side and roof of the structure.

I could then see through a large window of the warehouse where about four alien people were gathered around looking at a huge hanging chart that lit up with data at the touch of a button.

One was standing as if indicating specific points on the chart with a remote-control object. Then another one got up and seemed to be waving his hands with gestures of anger as if unhappy with progress.

Then they went outside towards the vault and one snapped as he opened it, "we need the gold and diamond inserts to effectively signal earth and locate the unknown." They were almost blinded by the sparkling light that shone on to the diamonds, and stepped back while placing their hands over their eyes.

We could see the vault clearly from our perch to the side of the huge wall as they proceeded to take a tray out containing some long gold bars, followed by a bag containing the prized diamonds.

These were placed alongside the gold bar, while the laser beam lights from the electronic birds in the tall tree shone down, everything sparkled. We had finally found the location of the prized diamonds but needed to investigate further.

Two other strange looking alien folk with spikes on their foreheads came by with a robot as the others were examining the diamonds, distracting them for their intended task to deal with some emergency. They all rushed back to the work area behind the high wall, but one alien returned to secure the vault and I almost got caught," said Jabokie.

"We had another narrow escape on our final day," said Jabokie. "Just as the juniors were being hurried back to the glass train, after their activities by two tall aliens. Billy the badger almost got caught as he came above ground to check measurements for the emergency tunnel leading to the vault.

One or two junior robots must have seen him, as a couple were pointing out of the glass train and more gathered to peer out. The aliens looked around and one went quickly to the activity area, as if checking to ensure nobody was left behind while the other looked after him impatiently as he checked his watch at the same time. They then signalled to the train to move away and by this time Billy the badger was out of view.

That was a nervous moment I can tell you and at the same time we were terrified they may have identified Sally the swallow while she tried to study and befriend the bird-like creatures beaming laser light onto the vault.

As Eddie the hedgehog hid close by waiting for the right moment to sniff around the control dial to the vault. Both were in extremely difficult and dangerous situations and even though they are good, they sometimes slip up in stressful situations.

We then had to break the code to the vault and extract the diamonds or what was left of them, while Sally distracted the two birds and interrupted their laser light view of the vault, as we desperately tried to disable the code. Eddie suddenly broke the code to the vault and the diamonds were finally in our possession. Everyone dashed to the assembly point and just as we were about to depart, the alarm to the vault went off. The entire area was blue with red sparks flying as we escaped in the magic arrow carriage under the cover of invisibility, otherwise, we would have been slain in an instant. And were lucky our magic powers work better in the dark so we could swiftly and safely escape," said Jabokie.

"Of course everyone was prepared and on high alert for this mission so there were hardly any mistakes apart from switching the alarm of the vault to zero instead of totally deactivating it and then closing the vault when we left, as it was most likely on a timer.

But hopefully rescuing your princess will not be such a complex operation even if she is being held captive on the Dark planet," said Jabokie.

"Then there was the panicked scientist who wanted our assistance to recover a secret miracle medicine formula after an explosion in his workshop destroyed the recipes for the medicine. An ancient tribe made the miracle medicine from secret recipes, passed down over generations, and cured disease in young and old alike. The medicinal plant medicine was used by the tribe to cure a range of local ailments like poisonous snakebites, fevers, skin conditions, set bones, act as a blood clotting agent, disinfectant and during tribal rituals.

The Tribe lived deep in the tropical rainforest and that too sounded like an exciting adventure, but was difficult beyond belief. As we were unable to use our usual woodland friends in the rescue and recovery mission, so we had to retreat a couple of hours after arriving, or we would all have been trapped, captured and killed by the large birds of prey, the huge snakes, crocodiles, cougars and other unfriendly folk who live deep in the tropical rain forest.

The environment of the tropical rainforest is tricky to navigate, as the landscape is so varied comprising of not just forest, but rivers and associated tributaries, floodplains and savannah and there are no signposts. So it's very easy to get lost in the dense forest, sucked under in the swamps, electrocuted or eaten in the rivers and their floodplains, or attacked in the open bush and grasslands of the savannah.

Sadly, we lost Eddie the Hedgehog's friend Herbert, who was carried away and devoured by large bird of prey, much bigger than any we know of. And Sally the swallow got almost suffocated by a giant speckled owl that pounced down from a higher branch of the dense

26

canopy of trees, trapping her. She possibly lost concentration while trying to avoid a green boa snake that was just inches away. Only for she used her beak to prod, pick, tickle and pinch the large owl, she would not have escaped.

"I firmly insisted that we retreat after a very rare loss of life and a near-miss Precious One," said Jabokie. "And that same rule will apply if we feel the situation is too dangerous and difficult, until we can figure out a better way of safely achieving our mission."

"Our next challenge was to explain the difficulties encountered on that initial fact-finding reconnaissance mission to the panicked scientist, whose first reaction was to throw his papers onto the floor in a red faced rage, when we tried to convince him to re-create the powerful medicinal medicine from the many other medicinal tropical plants and herbs growing in the region. Like the Pau d'Acro whose essence is widely used in herbal and traditional medicine, to treat malaria, diabetes, fungal infections and cancers. The bark of the cinchona tree whose essence is separated for immediate use by pharmaceutical companies.

Others like the Curare plant also has strong medicinal properties and used as a muscle relaxant during surgery, and to treat a number of other illnesses. The nutritious fruits of the Brazil nut tree are enjoyed globally, and so many more plant varieties are being screened for life saving medicines and used by the native tribes during various tribal rituals.

All such plant varieties are readily available for research and use, according to our sources, and maybe you will discover some new more powerful plant essence along the way," suggested Jabokie.

"However, such a solution did not impress or interest the impatient and anxious scientist, as he waved his hands helplessly in the air, appearing to get even more panicked. "All my work along with extensive research findings and laboratory tests are useless without the recipe for the miracle portion," pleaded the stressed scientist, as he stared vacantly into the distance beyond. It seemed as though nothing could replace what he lost," said Jabokie.

As his institution was awaiting samples from the miracle medicinal portion destroyed in the explosion and he simply had to find a way to reproduce this portion again – there were no alternatives.

Any other solution or suggestion for that matter, was useless in his view, as the powerful miracle formula was never used before outside the confines of the native tribes and their people. "I do not even have the recipes and cannot remember the ingredients ...I need the recipes to recreate the secret miracle medical formula," pleaded the very distressed red-faced scientist.

"I tried to explain that this would not be easy, as everyone was spooked from the initial fact-finding mission and not interested in any further adventure to the tropical rainforest until there was at least a better plan with reinforced supernatural powers and local contacts to guide us," said Jabokie.

"We knew it was time to retreat," said Jabokie to the Snow Queen, "when sadly Herbert the hedgehog didn't make it and Sally the swallow was shocked and nervous after her ordeal, despite her many expeditions through foreign lands during annual migration to Africa. But she just never expected to meet a green boa snake trying hard to catch frog in the tree branches and then get trapped inches from danger under the dense canopy.

Now you could say that maybe Sally lost concentration, got careless, confused or nervous as she sometimes does and we should have taken Freddie the falcon instead, as he adapts well to changing climates and can live in the Tundra or Tropical rainforest.
He and his family of Peregrine falcon folk are fast in the air and never miss catching their prey on the ground. But Freddie lacks judgement in dangerous situations, especially when the enemy or his prey is poisonous, stronger and much more dangerous than himself.

Or that Herbert the younger hedgehog was not concentrating or experienced enough and didn't have his favourite feed of snails for days, or maybe still in hibernation mode, which was abruptly cancelled.

And in hindsight we should have taken the otters, as they are clever on land and in water or Billy the badger and his friends, as they are careful and observant on the ground and can tunnel underground too.

Still the angry distressed scientist found it difficult to believe or imagine such a hostile, dangerous environment," said Jabokie.

Explaining his earlier research visit there as a young man travelling by jeep overland for three days with friendly guards and a guide.

"The most difficult part was the heat and the bumpy road which was at times just a mud track. We went during the dry season to avoid the heavy rain falls and floods," said the scientist, "which would have made our passage almost impossible. I had my briefing papers, and a guide book for reference - which I read before leaving and made a list of where and what to avoid," said the Scientist.

"And I knew there were four different levels within the tropical rain forest, starting at 'ground level', then the 'understory level', to the canopy level and finally the 'emergent level' found at the top of the tallest trees," explained the scientist, as he continued to recount details of an earlier visit to the tropical rain forest as a young student.

"I was aware of the many dangerous reptile creatures lurking in the swamps, and saw a huge alligator sunning itself by the edge of a lake or flood plain as we went by.
According to my guidebook, in the streams and muddy waters, we could expect to see other very dangerous reptiles like the aquatic coral snakes, whose bite is venomous. Other snakes from the reptile family, like the giant anaconda and boa constrictor were more of a worry, as they are usually found at the 'ground' and the 'understory' levels of the tropical rainforest. As are most of the large mammals like jaguars, cougars and less dangerous tapir, but thankfully we encountered no such creatures," said the scientist.

"As we journeyed deeper into the forest, the mud track almost disappeared and I remember we lost a half-day clearing away some fallen trees and debris blocking our onward journey.

At 'ground level', the forest floor is the darkest of all rain forest layers, making it extremely difficult for plants to grow there. Leaves fall to the forest floor and decay quickly with the help of insect decomposers, such as termites, slugs, scorpions, and worms that break down the decaying material into nutrients. The shallow roots of the trees then absorb these nutrients.

We did see army ants at one point but they are difficult to miss, as hundreds of thousands travel together hunting for food for their larvae. I also expected to see some leaf cutter ants, as their name suggests, they collect various leafs and take them to their underground nest, but none appeared.

According to our guide, some insects use defence mechanisms, like the bullet ants that sting predators and the giant millipede insects emit a poisonous toxin. Others like the stick insects use a strong camouflage for protection against predators, as they pursue their daily routine. According to my guidebook, I could expect to also see bess beetles, ground beetles, jewel beetles, hunter spiders, bird-eating spiders and cockroaches, but none were visible as we cleared away the debris and mud blocking our path.

While our driver and guides continued to clear the debris, I had some time then to get a closer look around which was more difficult from the bumpy moving jeep.

But at this point, I remember being more worried we might encounter some larger dangerous mammals at ground floor level, like the panther orca, cougars or gorillas and would have no chance of escape.

The 'understory level' of the tropical rainforest is darker and cooler, and wildlife species are less varied at this level. Plants such as palms and philodendrons, the cercopia trees, lianas and vines are much shorter but have larger leaves to catch the minimal rays of sunlight that reaches through the dense tropical rainforest.

At the 'understory level', I also saw some rheas and ostriches, in the undergrowth but they disappeared quickly as I came closer, as did the peccaries and agoutis, so I did not get any pictures. Some tamaduas also appeared briefly to enjoy their usual feast of slugs and termites. And hiding in the tall and short tropical grasses and sticky plants at the 'understory level' of the tropical rain forest are also chameleons, scorpions, snakes and may more predatory animals.

Higher up at the 'canopy level', some brightly coloured flowers also appeared through the trees and they were surrounded by hummingbirds with the longest beaks I have ever seen. Our guide said the flowers were lobster claw heliconia's flowers and the hummingbirds were helping themselves to the sweet nectar from the flowers. I was surprised to see an abundance of orchids dotted around along with the Purple flowered Glory bush and Bromeliads trees.

There were brightly coloured butterflies like the malachite, glass wing butterfly and swallowtail butterfly with red markings that emits toxic chemicals as a defence, according to my guidebook.

We heard a couple of howler monkeys in the overhead branches sounding panicked, and caught a glimpse of a few sloths as they swung from branch to branch using their claws. Further along, some spider monkeys also emerged hanging upside down by their long tails as they moved from branch to branch, even though difficult to see through the dense canopy of tree foliage. I did however manage to catch a glimpse of a margay cat who disappeared instantly from view in the upper canopy of trees as the sound of intruders.

In fact, the majority of wildlife species are found at the 'canopy level' of the tropical rain forest, because there is sunlight, warmth, moisture and food in abundance, so I was a little disappointed I didn't get more pictures," explained the scientist.

"At highest point of the tropical rainforest or 'emergent level', I thought I saw a harpy eagle in the taller Monkey Puzzle trees or Mahogany trees which were in abundance, as were the huge Brazil nut trees, and ancient Cacao trees that were laden with cocoa beans.

As we gained altitude, there were some podocarpus trees also at the 'emergent level'. From time to time, various multi-coloured birds flew from the tree branches as we journeyed through the forest. I could hear loud callings further along that disrupted the sudden silence.

Our guide said they sounded like toucan or maybe the scarlet, yellow or blue macaws, but hard to tell, as the tropical rainforest is home to so many species of multi-coloured birds, like the various coloured Macaws and others like the Hoatzins, Grey Headed Kite, Lesser Yellowlegs, Parrots, Trogons and Armadillos.

Some birds are even too big to fly, or simply don't fly like the Peacocks, Jabiru Storks, Ostriches and Rheas. Others I agree are dangerous in the air and on the ground like eagles and the Viper Bat from the mammal family that spreads disease such as malaria and rabies," explained the scientist, as he continued to recount details of his earlier journey.

"We had to hike for about an hour with some supplies in the absences of a road or even a mud track in the sweltering heat, through tall and short tropical grasses at the understory and ground levels of the dense forest. And onwards through the open bush-lands of the savannah, to the meeting place by the river.

We then boarded a dugout canoe, where two brightly painted and scantily clad men from the remote native tribe were waiting to take us down river. The river and tributaries serve as an efficient highway for folks in the tropical rain forest.

As we journeyed down river, I remember seeing some river dwelling creatures like the giant otter and four or five young appeared along side. I was surprised to see some river dolphins as we passed a waterfall, and in the deeper part of the river some other very large fish appeared, according to our guide, they were piraracu arapauma. We then saw a huge menatee, which was hard to miss, as they are also the largest mammals in South America and even though they are river dwelling mammals, they have to eat vast amounts of plant matter during the wet season to survive throughout the dry season.

As we continued down river, I saw some large rodents on the riverbank, also known as cybabara, according to my guidebook.
I caught a glimpse of a black caymen crocodile on the muddy part of the riverbank and further along a tapir had just emerged from the water, close to some wading birds who had moved further inland to the surrounding wetlands for the dry season.

During the journey by canoe, we passed crystal waterfalls, went through caves and narrow ravines, to finally reach our meeting point which was about another thirty minutes on foot through the forest, whose dense canopy and overhanging foliage at times blocked out the sky, but there was no threatening situation.

So Jabokie, I find it very difficult to believe with your skill and magic powers you had difficulty or encountered such danger," said the scientist.

"This is true, but every mission is different and you possibly weren't aware of the many dangers, were careful and had the protection of native guards and a guide to assist you on that journey, which I assure you makes everything more pleasant and enjoyable my good Sir," said Jabokie.

"You must understand, the forest has been under attack in more recent times," said Jabokie. "How do you mean," asked the scientist. "Well there has been mass deforestation, caused by illegal loggers, cattle herders extending their ranches for livestock and planting crops of soya. Such practices have forced the native tribes to abandon their homes, as their traditional hunting grounds have now disappeared along with plants and animal wildlife.

Illegal mining and oil and gas drilling has also damaged the natural environment, leaving a toxic residue of chemicals that seeps under the soil and poisons the water. Then the various dam development projects for hydroelectric and industrial purposes also impact negatively.

Such developments have changed the forest environment for native tribes as well as animal and plant life, forcing everyone to fight for safety and survival. So, it's no surprise really we encountered such hostile and dangerous folk," explained Jabokie.

"Maybe they also sensed our magic powers and as you know there are so many different species of animals, birds and plants under and over the dense canopy of the tropical forest. Making it impossible to sneak in without a very effective camouflage or help from native tribes.
Even with a great camouflage, inside back-up and listings from our own guide books, we had to avoid dangerous members of the reptile family as you mentioned like the boa constrictor, the black snakes, red snakes and green snakes. Along with other species from the amphibian family like, the pink frogs, tree frogs, and poison frogs like the dart frog and smoking jungle frogs. Along with electric eels that shock, shoals of

piranha fish that will attack and kill if unlucky enough to encounter during a mission in water," said Jabokie.

"On land, dangerous mammals like the cougar, and jaguar whose name translates as 'he who kills in one leap', can suddenly appear, even though you are less likely to meet or see them now, as they have moved due to the land reclamation and illegal logging. But they are perhaps even more dangerous as their habitat and food supply has been disrupted and in many cases destroyed.

Some animal and bird folk are quiet but no less dangerous as you said, others loud and alarming if encountered on a day or night mission as they can alert the enemy, along with the thousands of animals, plants and native tribes not yet discovered by the outside world, and the list goes on," said Jabokie to the Snow Queen. So surprise, alarm, fear and danger await on almost every mission, and especially so under such a dense canopy of forest trees. The open bush-land of the savannahs is also dangerous, as your team is more exposed, therefore extra protection and backup is necessary, so it's difficult to decide on the perfect plan and approach," explained Jabokie.

"Seasonal changes and weather conditions are important considerations and determines who is available to assist and easy to reach especially in places like a tropical rainforest. During the dry season, which lasts for six months, the deciduous trees lose their leaves and there is less shelter, so some animals' species like cats, lizards, iguanas and many more will move away to areas where food is more plentiful.

In the wet season, which also lasts for six months, certain species of birds like the fish eagle, some vultures and a variety of wading birds will migrate or move further inland or to higher ground.

Others species reproduce at this time, so they are busy tending to their young, and therefore not available to assist us.

Making it so difficult to plan for each strange, dangerous and unexpected encounter, not to mention getting submerged in a swamp, falling down a ravine or lost in the vast forest, with only danger to keep you company. And not all our woodland friends can work in such a hot tropical environment.

As a result, we were forced to change our approach and this is where our communication network 'Helloland' was especially useful, otherwise our mission would not have been possible.

And even though it took more time and careful planning to put a smart team together to accomplish our mission, we were finally successful," said Jabokie.

"Then there was our adventure to the Ice planet," said Jabokie. "Yes," said the Snow Queen, "this really impressed my people, especially how your magic powers released Santa's helpers who got stuck by melting ice."

"That is true," said Jabokie, "Santa's helpers had got stuck during an exploration mission and we had to free them. We picked up their distress signal from 'Helloland'. A huge iceberg blocked their secret mission passage back to Santa's workshop and were at risk of an evil invasion to steal their secret cargo from lists for many children around the globe from the leaking ship that was now starting to sink," said Jabokie.

"That was also a very difficult mission Precious One, as we had to make so many changes because not everyone could survive the ice and snow, even with magic powers.
We then had to wait for the additional reinforcement of reindeers to arrive even though some couldn't make it as they were too far away gathering toys and new ideas for Santa's workshop and one got lost," recounted Jabokie.

"The Caribous wanted to stay close to their young and some had moved away because of the oil and gas drilling close to their grazing areas.

The walrus were too slow even with magic powers and could only be useful as a distraction. The white fox family were suspicious and distant from the start, unwilling to risk such danger; the snow owls needed convincing, the hare's were nervous and complained about the air and ground dangers and the constant threats to their world.

The polar bears were fine, but there were fewer to choose from at that time as they had moved further away to avoid getting stranded with the melting ice. Climate change meant the warmer water was melting the snow and ice, forcing many animals to move in search of food and a new home.

We were shocked to see the once solid frozen snow covered ground had now melted and disappeared in places, so we had to choose our new path carefully.

The penguins seemed panicked by events and difficult to organise as there were so many, but our best bet. Even then, some weren't quite right, as they couldn't concentrate and stay focused to guard the area, while we desperately tried to save the cargo and remove it from the damaged and now sinking ship. We were lucky the Arctic eagles and Peregrine falcons were sharp, alert and knew the area very well, so could alert us to danger while we waited for the additional reindeer and sleighs to arrive.

Just as we were about to return from that mission, we had to try and rescue two polar bear cubs who were stranded on a little island of melting snow close to where Santa's helpers were struck.

The older polar bears had just pushed through the huge blocks of melting snow and ice, but the cubs were not strong enough. The penguins were useful here as they were familiar and didn't frighten the cubs as we tried to get them safely onto dry ground.

The impact of warming waters due to climate change had totally disrupted life for the polar bears and seals on both land and sea, forcing them to swim further out into the ocean for food, or move to higher ground further inland for safety and shelter.

At the same time, we received news that another one of Santa's helpers misread the instructions on his map, took a wrong turn and was lost way out there in the universe, high above the clouds.

This was an urgent and stressful mission, as he seemed so very far away. Nobody knew where this planet was or how we would reach its location to rescue Santa's lost helper and reindeers.

We asked the moon if there were any sightings, but the response was negative and suggested we check with the planets in the inner and outer universe, as she was focused and shining on planet Earth.
So we tried to search and signal through 'Helloland', starting with the inner planets; the first one, even though closest to the sun, was hard to see and appeared covered in fog, the next planet was very bright and visible from earth, but still no response from either," recounted Jabokie.

"When we finally managed to make contact, he told us he was on a red planet with only large craters in the ground and some rocks scattered around the flat red dusty surface. He could see a very tall mountain in the distance and a pink silver sky above. Otherwise, everything looked the same, as he waited by some rocks with nothing or nobody in sight. That was such a relief to hear, as we knew Santa's lost helper wasn't in immediate danger. But were aware and on alert this situation could change and hostile alien life emerge on the red planet, were he to remain there for too long and his oxygen mask might also cease to be effective," explained Jabokie.

We were lucky Santa's helper wasn't lost on the outer planets, as my sources tell me it would have taken so much longer to reach and rescue him, as some of these planets are bigger. One is surrounded by rings of dust and ice, another surrounded by an ocean, a blue planet with a rocky surface that orbits on its side and a planet that is completely frozen over. So even with magic powers, all would be extremely difficult to navigate.

We then had to contact Santa's head office in Lapland, get the map for the correct route and with the help of 'Helloland' communication signals, try to guide Santa's lost helper and loaded sleigh safely back to earth," explained Jabokie.

"There are always delays and complications in getting the right team together that could work in the snow and ice, a tropical rainforest or a distant dark planet," said Jabokie.
"Well this time you would of course have my army at your disposal and I myself will assist however I can, with a reasonable ransom or reward for a successful outcome," said the Snow Queen.
"We need to find my princess as quickly as possible and I fear we have already wasted too much time," said the panicked Snow Queen.

"Oh my Precious One let's not talk about rewards just yet as this is a very dangerous and serious mission into unknown lands and who knows what the outcome is likely to be or even where the enemy hails from. So we must act urgently, as my intuition tells me she may be in grave danger," said Jabokie.

"Oh dear, I must get back, as my carriage will soon start to melt here and I will then also be disabled in your climate. But before I leave, can you help me Jabokie? "I need to know as you are the only one I can trust now," said the distressed and anxious Snow Queen.

"Let me see, first of all, I will have to cancel or postpone hibernation, then enact the magic transforming spell on our secret special mission army. Even then, we still must find the enemy, establish their strength, size, distract them and rescue your princess," said Jabokie.

"I have not disclosed the true nature of our distress for fear the enemy in other kingdoms would seek advantage and maybe strike, especially if our army is preoccupied elsewhere. Do you understand? – So, this must remain a top-secret mission," said the Snow Queen – "I agree," said Jabokie.

"Our plans and movements have to remain a total secret even to those in our woodland world, who will not be joining the mission. We will just be exploring other lands of opportunity for new ideas and treasure, to increase our woodland comforts and lifestyle - that's it, no further explanation will be given or indeed required," said Jabokie.

"Do you have any images or drawings of these people, symbols or markings that would help us identify their origins," asked Jabokie. "I can tell you they had two stars and a spike on their forehead," said the Snow Queen. "There is no question, whatever land they come from, they are powerful," said Jabokie.

"The mission can be difficult on a dark or hostile planet, as we have to change colour to blend in,   even though we are more powerful in darkness. The direct attack may work best when we discover their location or planet, but if this doesn't work, we may have to negotiate," said Jabokie.

"How do you mean," asked the Snow Queen. "Well if we don't have the treasure they so desperately seek, we will have to negotiate the release of your princess," said Jabokie. "So, we need a plan or idea to somehow get the princess back," said Jabokie. "What were you thinking of," asked the Snow Queen. "Well depending on where your princess is or on what planet – we will then spread the word," said Jabokie. "My friend, this has to remain a top secret mission," said the Snow Queen anxiously.

"This is true, but my network will have to be told, as I will need them to support our powers. Our people now have contacts on almost every planet through our secret technology system 'Helloland'. This allows us to finally communicate with our network of contacts and make friends in every part of the world. We can link up with neighbours next door, or interested parties in the Jungle, desert, mountains and valleys and help them out if in difficulty, or get their assistance when we need it," said Jabokie.

"In the jungle, even though there are several thousand different species to call upon, some are extremely dangerous without any magic spell at all, others will not be suitable as they are too slow, have difficulty blending in, are hard to camouflage and cannot follow instructions or worse still want to make their own rules," said Jabokie.

"For example: we have mountain lions, grizzly bears and wolfs in the mountains and hyenas, jaguars and cougars in the savannah and forest, crocodiles and poisonous snakes in the swamps, streams, rivers and wetlands, all very powerful creatures and their power is doubled with our magic spell. Of course, we have to be careful who we select and can trust, which we've learned from our various expeditions," said Jabokie to the Snow Queen.

"Let us waste no more time, I will send out "an all stars flashing red alert" message to our network, which indicates a most urgent search situation with immediate action required.
This way we will have thousands looking for unknown warriors, watching strange movements and listening for talk of lost treasure in their area or planet," said Jabokie.

"We will also send a false or trick message and its symbol 'dancing stars' to try and catch the enemy. 'Lost Treasure from unknown planet found but princess still missing. Can you help'!
This may lead us quickly to those who kidnapped your princess," explained Jabokie. "Otherwise we will have to search and then if we find these unknown alien warriors, decide whether to attack them directly or trick them into releasing your princess by negotiating an exchange for our beautiful goddess of night. After all, she is beautiful, skilful and talented, with additional superpowers when I transfer the magic spell.

Which by the way will only last for a while, but the evil ones will not know this? So, the trick will be to exchange our goddess of darkness there in the trees, for your princess.

"Such magic powers will also lull them into a deep stupor. So we can then escape with your princess and will have returned her safely when the evil invaders wake up and realize they have been fooled. We will put the plan into action first light and depart as darkness falls on our land in the evening. We will contact you as soon as we have news of your princess and her captors," said Jabokie.

"Do you think it will work," asked the nervous Snow Queen. "I think it most definitely will," repied Jabokie, "especially after I transfer magic powers, promising that the goddess of darkness can ward off evil and find the lost treasure." "I think it's a marvellous idea," agreed the Snow Queen.
"We have to try every possible means to find and rescue my little princess, and I trust you Jabokie, as I know your missions are always successful," said the anxious Snow Queen.

"I knew from my dream as I woke up panicked and frightened that I had to rescue my dolly urgently, before they took her to faraway lands, cast magic spells, and put my dolly in great danger," recounted Susie.

"So, I decided to go quickly to the tree house to try and rescue her. But I didn't think it was so far away when I saw it in the distance earlier, as we all walked down the winding path.

When I got to the tree house, I could see my dolly hanging from a branch by the window at the top and climbed up the wooden stairs to try to rescue her. As I went up to the second level of the tree house, the door slammed shut and the rusty latch jammed," explained Susie.

"Oh dear," sighed Mrs Condry, "what a terrible dream that suddenly became a nightmare for everyone especially if we hadn't found you.
"Can you help me get my dolly from the branch at the top by the window ledge now," asked Susie. "Oh Ok," said Mrs Condry.

"Farmer Fred, Farmer Fred," called out Mrs Condry and he turned around at once.
"Will you bring the ladder back please, we now also have to rescue Susie's dolly too. She is suspended at the top of the tree house by the window ledge." "Sure thing," said Fred. He then climbed the ladder to perform his second rescue mission of the stranded dolly.

After a little tugging with one hand to untangle the dress caught in the branches, Fed finally rescued the doll, came back down the ladder and gave her to a delighted Susie.

4

WOODLAND AND WILDLIFE

The woodland is also home to many species of wildlife like hedgehogs, foxes, minks, badgers, stoats, rabbits, hares, varieties of birds, bee communities, flies and butterflies and their many insect and mini-beast friends found in the undergrowth and soil. Even though you don't see them very often, they all live in tranquillity and harmony with nature, winter, spring, summer and autumn.

Their peace and quiet only disturbed by occasional intruders and the sound of water gushing down river after heavy rainfall. Mrs Mallery said the weekend was the worst time in the woodlands for all the tiny animals, birds and plants, especially when the grouse and pheasant season starts in autumn.

Hunters come on shoots at various times, as there is an abundance of game birds like pheasant, grouse, along with varieties of wild fowl like wood pigeon, curlew, golden plover, teal and snipe in the surrounding meadows, woodlands, pasturelands and wetlands. Such birds were also treasured for their tender tasting meat, and appeared on most shopping lists, for banquets in the 17th and 18th century.

"The annual hunt must also be a terrifying time for the woodland family," said Adrianna. Folks on horses and ponies arrive in varied coloured riding attire, with a dozen or more hounds racing alongside. As they gallop through fields, woodlands and meadows, speedily jumping over every wall and fences as if invisible, with an ever-increasing urgency to catch the cunning fox or hare and on the odd occasion appears to succeed, while making lots of noise in the process.

The fox can be a pest on farm land, frequently steeling hens, ducks and lambs to feed its young, but was also treasured in years gone by for its pelt which was used in garment manufacturing. It is said that the fox family have survived for 5000 years because of their cunning nature and ability to sense danger, thereby avoiding capture.

The hunt party often stop by the river to rest and water the horses, before moving off quickly again to the sound of a bellowing horn that summons the hounds and orders the horses, for the onward chase through woodlands and pasturelands in search of the elusive fox before heading home. Peace and tranquillity returns once again to woodland life for everyone not least the cleaver fox.

One time after breakfast as three friends went for their usual morning run in the grass; a big brown rabbit suddenly appeared outside the vegetable patch. Buddy chased after the rabbit as he raced through the pastureland followed by Bow and Perry the poodle close behind. The Mrs Moos, Mrs Sheep and their young raced in the opposite direction to escape the urgent chase.

I need the magic lasso thought Buddy as he instantly raced back to the gate to get it, while Bow and Perry the poodle continued to chase the speedy brown rabbit.

As they reached the meadow, the rabbit was quickly escaping in the long grass that slowed them down. With that, Buddy cast the magic lasso hoping to catch the speedy brown rabbit.

Buddy then felt a kind of tugging on the lasso and was certain he had caught the speedy brown rabbit, but as he came closer, discovered he had instead caught Mother goose, who was now choking and could hardly breathe with the tight lasso round her neck and her wings frantically flapping in panic.

Buddy quickly released Mother Goose, who raced over to join her young. Two other ducks from the Muscovy and Quail families crouched down with their young goslings in the long grass. All appearing shocked and frightened by the sudden attack on their routine morning stroll though the meadow to the nearby pond. Where they went most mornings while helping themselves along the way to the unsuspecting worms who were busy tunnelling into their home in the ground which also helps to irrigate and drain the soil. Along with their many insect neighbours hiding in the long grasses like the stag beetles, centipedes and earwigs whose work in decomposing waste material also helped to fertilise the soil and aid re-growth, but all were shocked beyond belief by events.

Even members of the butterfly family like the red admiral, tortoiseshell, ringlet, dark green fritillary, speckled wood, and peacock butterfly, who usually take time to silently show off their bright colours, resting on the long grasses and flowering posies moved on quickly. As did various members of the fly family like the hover fly, dragon fly, blue bottle, midge and others who usually make their presence known buzzing in the tall grasses, or through their bite, along with the crickets and ladybirds, but all were alarmed and gave space to the urgent chase. Leaping, flying and creeping with urgency in every direction to avoid the sudden and frightening disruption to their world. Buddy felt very foolish indeed and quickly removed the lasso from a very shocked Mother goose.

Carlos the crow and friends gathered in the high oak tree with Margie magpie. Robbie the robin, Sally the sparrow, skylark, the wagtails and thrushes looked on in silence from the nearby hawthorn trees at the three friends' frantic act to catch the speedy rabbit, who at this point had escaped through the hedge close to the woodland wall.

Suddenly, a large community of bees emerged startling the three friends. And more followed, buzzing loudly around the friends distracting and stopping their urgent effort to catch the big brown rabbit.

Soon there were hundreds of buzzing bees around and it was difficult to determine who the queen bee or worker bees were, or if they belonged to the Honeybee or Bumblebee or other species of the bee family, as they were moving around so fast. Buddy heard Adrianna explain the difference once before, and decided these were not bumblebees as the bumblebee colony comprises of just 50 to 200 bees, and their hive is found in an old mice burrow, or crevice in the wall where they hibernated in winter.

Whereas the honeybees' colony is a swarm, just like this one and their hive is a much more complex interwoven affair, where the honey is manufactured from the nectar collected by the bees in the summer, and stored for winter.

The honeybees were domesticated in olden times, because they produced honey in sufficient quantities for humans to harvest and bees wax. The honey was used to sweeten food and drinks, in fact, honey is one of the oldest sweetening agents as it was used long before sugar and spices were available in many countries.

In ancient folklore, the bee was considered a wise, industrious and organised creature; and was associated with the goddess of abundance and fertility of the land. Possibly because the bees were relied upon to pollinate plants, ensuring continuous re-growth.

Even so, who would have thought such little creatures would have ended our race to catch the naughty brown rabbit thought Buddy.

As the bee community returned to the task of repairing their damaged beehive, Buddy, Bow and Perry the poodle slowly and cautiously returned once again to the peace and quiet of their world with the naughty brown rabbit beyond their reach.

Buddy then started to wonder where the speedy rabbit lived, and if he would ever succeed in catching him. Next time will be different thought Buddy, I will investigate when I go out to explore in the meadow and woodland.

My special project will be to find where the brown rabbit lives thought Buddy - maybe discover his trail. I will then lay in wait and pounce as soon as he appears. In fact, I know for definite he lives in a warren in the woodland.

Therefore, I will avoid the long grasses of the meadow, the waddling ducks and their young, the angry bees in their beehive by the woodland wall and take a shorter cut to the woods. Who knows, maybe the speedy brown rabbit deliberately lead us to the beehive, knowing exactly what would happen when thousands of honeybees were disturbed.

This is a trap I will not jump into or be lead into again, thought Buddy. I will be smarter and discover exactly where the clever rabbit lives. So I will know the precise direction to take next time. Bow and Perry will not be interested in 'next time', after their narrow escape from the swarm of angry bees.

And even if they did venture again they would probably repeat the same mistake - so this will be my project alone, thought Buddy. I will have a plan and rehearsed my moves for next time. The naughty brown rabbit is out of luck if the thinks he can munch away in the cabbage patch, trip us up with his swift escape and get away with it.

Later on that evening after tea, as the friends rested and then dozed off to a deep slumber...in his dreams, Buddy entered another world with bunny rabbits, little boys and girls at play, and party plans in motion. Buddy was paralysed by fear among Mrs Bunny rabbit and her clan.

It was a weird experience and in a hazy blur... Buddy was suddenly falling down the speedy Rabbit's burrow. Not sure I am safe even though I may have finally discovered where the speedy rabbit and his friends live...I have finally succeeded... Buddy was met at the end of a flower lined path by a little girl holding a tray of delicious chocolate chip cookies under a huge tree. The tree had a door with a long latch; there were two windows on either side above the door with yellow and white curtains.

The little girl then went inside and the door swayed open at the same time, so Buddy, eager as always to explore and especially if mystery and intrigue await, followed cautiously, sniffing the ground in the usual way, but was then transfixed with the sweet aroma of baked cookies.

Buddy went down a little entrance hall where the wall was covered with pictures of Bunny rabbits young and old, large and small. He then went through a small door, where he saw a table with all his favourite treats and was so very tempted to try some hazelnut and honey cookies.

Further along on a large sideboard, were blackberry, rhubarb, blackcurrant, gooseberry, apple and plumb pies, all clearly labelled. He could also see carrot cake, apple and honey cake, beetroot cake, and potato cakes that all looked delicious and Buddy desperately wanted to taste some.

This idea was abandoned when he heard the sound of footsteps, startled; he hid under the table and stayed very still.

The footsteps were followed by a gaggle of little screeching voices, who were silenced by a more serious older sounding voice giving orders, which he didn't understand. He continued to stay still to avoid alerting anyone to his presence, as he was an uninvited guest, and more seriously, an unwelcome intruder.

Buddy now wished he had stayed outside and played with the little girl and her friends who he could now hear singing, she was now joined by a couple of other friends and they were skipping and playing ball on the path. My need to explore is not always wise, thought Buddy – I should be more careful!

From his position under the table, he could see at least four bunny rabbits with aprons, some chopping a selection of root vegetables, like carrots, parsnips, turnip and onion, others were chopping some leafy vegetables, like cabbage, lettuce and spinach. Mrs Bunny Rabbit was close by stirring a large pot of stew on a stove and checking the other treats that were baking in the oven.

There were overhead shelves with jars labelled 'Cooking herbs'. One jar contained parsley, there were also jars containing mint, sage, thyme and coriander. On the top shelve there was a large sign that read 'Medicinal herbs', with jars of lavender, nettle, ribwort, dandelion, horse chestnut, lemongrass, comfrey, rosehip, garlic, blackberries, willow, wood anemone peppermint and fennel.

On the middle shelf, there were jars of honey, hazelnut and honey syrup, blackcurrant, and blackberry jam, elderberry juice and a huge treat box with hazelnut cookies and roasted horse chestnut toffee lollypops.

Everyone appeared to have a job in preparation for the party. Other footsteps came through the door and they were louder. It was the little girl he had met outside asking Mrs Rabbit what time the party was starting at. "Oh, Mariella there you are, I heard you singing earlier - hopefully it's in preparation for the picnic and party," said Mrs Bunny Rabbit.

"The picnic will start at the later time of 3pm as our cousins from the other side of the lake are also coming. They have been delayed due to repair work on their house which got flooded by the heavy rain,and the party will start at 7pm," said Mrs Bunny Rabbit.

"So really we have plenty of time but so much work to do", said Mrs Bunny rabbit – "the cake is almost ready. Have some juice Mariella – that's a beautiful party dress you are wearing today!"

Buddy could then hear little voices interrupt saying "Mariella, will you play with us"? "Oh please Mariella, let's play catch like last time at Bertie's."

"My friends and I are playing a skipping game at the moment," said Mariella, "after we want to make a wigwam to play in during the party and you can come with us to help." "We have much more to do here too," said Mrs Rabbit as she opened the door to a long kitchen area.

Everyone appeared to have a job in preparation for the party. The little voices again pleading with Mariella, saying, "Oh please Mariella, can we come with, we promise to be very quiet and stay with you?"

"Ok ok, but first I have to find my new found friend," said Mariella. "And who is that," said a voice that sounded like Mrs Rabbit from the long kitchen.

"A puppy," replied Mariella ..."A puppy did you say," replied a startled, wide-eyed Mrs Rabbit in a louder panicked voice. ..."Yes...a puppy," said an uncertain Mariella.

Silence descended and Mrs Rabbit moved closer to Mariella. Buddy was getting nervous too...why
Mariella did you have to mention me thought Buddy? How will I escape now and what will I do if they discover my presence, which is about to happen anytime soon?
"Mariella, I am asking you again, where did you meet your new puppy friend?" ...Here!" said Mariella in a weakening little voice. "Here," said a panicked Mrs Rabbit...you mean outside in the woodlands... on the way!" ... No here at your house!" replied Mariella - "I thought he was early for the party and gave him some cookies like the ones I brought here earlier."

"Mariella why on earth did you think a puppy would ever be a welcome guest at our party," said Mrs Bunny Rabbit, "but I thought," said Mariella ...well think again Mariella, puppies are not our friends," said now very distressed Mrs Bunny Rabbit. "Puppies and their entire breed hunt our people and try to kill them. And if they discover where we live, well I dread to think of the outcome," said Mrs Bunny Rabbit.

"Young lady, you have no idea of the great danger we are now in ... You have to be smart and realise, you will always meet some wonderful people in life and make great friends too, but not everyone you meet is going to be your friend Mariella," said a panicked Mrs Bunny Rabbit... Where did your puppy friend go," asked Mrs Bunny Rabbit. "I'm not sure," said Mariella.

"Why do you think we have a reinforced basement with a playroom for the little bunny rabbits and months of food supplies in storage? That's not just for rainy days you know, it's for safety," said Mrs Bunny Rabbit.

"Harold will not be back either until end of the month - what should we do?" sighed a now whimpering Mrs Rabbit ... "I cannot even get to Heather across the way in Middlewood as it would not be safe. And with that Mrs Rabbit started to weep ... And Cristobel's babies are due anytime soon, so she cannot be disturbed," said a still whimpering Mrs Bunny Rabbit.

And our clever warriors Bartle and Julp who would race through the woodlands and warn folks with the thudding sound of their urgent movement, are out searching for a suitable warren for their ever increasing families," said a hopeless sounding Mrs Bunny Rabbit.

"And where's Skylark? ...He is always hovering for crumbs and sweet goodies when I don't need him.   I am going to have to send a message now to warn everyone. Maybe ask Margie the Magpie to deliver a warning sound to Heather and friends in Middlewood," said Mrs Bunny Rabbit.

"What about the picnic and party," asked a voice from the centre of preparation in the long kitchen. "Enough about the celebrations until we find the dangerous puppy impostor who is lurking in our mist waiting to pounce, with the possibility of many casualties... and the perfect opportunity, as we gather for party celebrations," said a panicked Mrs Rabbit.

"Oh there you are Skylark...quickly ...take this to our cousins at the lake... I have to warn them of the danger lurking in our mist...tell them to wait until after 5pm or closer to teatime," said Mrs Bunny Rabbit.

"Ok," said Skylark, with wings flapping as he bounced back and forth on the windowsill...I will now take your message urgently...how many puppies do you think are there," asked Skylark.
Only one that we know about," said Mrs Rabbit panicked stricken...but others may follow if he has discovered where we live!"

"Oh ...I will check as I go... from my birds' eye view of the entire woodland, whoever is hiding or trespassing will be seen. I will also tell

Margie Magpie and her friends, Carlos the crow and his flock will also watch from the giant oak and sycamore trees...so do not worry... I will spread the word quickly – nothing will escape our eyes Mrs Bunny Rabbit." "Oh call me Bunny Bow and thank you Skylark."

"Just sit tight, lock all the doors and windows and keep everyone inside until you get our signal," chirped Skylark. "Wonderful, what a relief, Henrietta in Middlewood and her folk will know and don't forget our cousins by the lake!" said Mrs Bunny Rabbit. "Sure thing," said Skylark. "Everyone will be alerted and warned of the imminent danger."

"Children do you hear me, everyone go at once to the basement." "Quickly children," said Mrs Rabbit, and at that moment, everyone descended to the basement. Buddy then raced towards the door, but couldn't open it – next thing Mariella appeared again..."there you are - we must leave immediately, but first I have to put this on you, said Mariella." Buddy's heart was racing – he would have climbed up the wall to the open window and taken his chances, in a desperate effort to escape. Crouching down whimpering as Mariella placed a dark cover over his eyes and tied it tightly.

This is much worse than the muzzle thought Buddy as his world disappeared in an instant and he was just moving along in darkness. A voice called out "Mariella...Mariella, where are you?"..."we must find your new friend." But Mariella's footsteps quickened as she continued to lead Buddy through what first seemed like a stony passage, onto short grass, and then through longer grass. He could hear Mariella open a gate and she then removed the cover from Buddy's eyes.

Buddy yelped out a cry of joy as his world returned once more...he now had to get back to Bow and Perry, and wondered which direction to take. He would leave quickly before Mariella came back, as he did not want to walk into another trap again for some time. He felt scared and exhausted by his moment in the world of bunny rabbits ...I still cannot believe I got so close thought Buddy.

Suddenly the loud calling of Carlos the crow and friends in the nearby trees awakened Buddy, even though he was still in a slightly dazed and confused state, the sight of Bow and Perry across the way staring back, made Buddy realise he was safely back home.

With hundreds of distraught bunnies on red alert running for cover, a nervous and almost tearful little girl, abandoned worktops full of yet to be enjoyed goodies for what appeared to be a ruined party. And everyone on high alert to the impeding
danger, or other imagined woes that Buddy represented in this dream... that fast became a nightmare for the bunny rabbits in their woodland world.

Why was I so afraid, when everything I planned and hoped for in catching the speedy rabbit was within reach - in fact only centimetres away, thought Buddy as he retreated, resting his head on his paws as if trying to comprehend events.

Why...why – I cannot share my dream with anyone as they would laugh and say I was crazy thought Buddy. Who would let such an opportunity go...? Even to avail of some cookies... and that stew... it smelled so amazing? Bow, Perry or even Felix the cat would have been more successful in such a situation without any plan at all.

Therefore, I will not mention anything, besides it was my plan and then in a deep slumber imagined all sorts of things. I am still so angry the speedy rabbit managed to trick us and escape last time.

5

REGGIE THE ROBOT

The strangest addition of all to the three friend's world was the arrival of Reggie the Robot. Simon got his dream birthday present – a Robot, more specifically Reggie the lifestyle Robot. Meaning Reggie had the ability to adapt and perform all sorts of useful tasks when functioning normally.

Reggie the robot brought everything to a standstill, as almost everyone in his universe ran for cover leaving just a deathly silence.

There was no sign of the other friendly and unfriendly neighbours unless in the distance or from a safely positioned vantage point, as Reggie the Robot randomly trooped about.

Reggie intrigued and at times spooked the three friends as he was unpredictable erratic and very strange with lights flashing in his eyes which were like laser beams at night.

If Reggie happened to become stuck or was approaching danger like a fire, steps or a steep incline, then the bleeps would become more frequent and louder, until finally an alarm sounded and Reggie's colour changed to red.

And he was totally scary if he appeared after dark when the three friends were going to sleep. With a squeaky noise and blue laser eyes that flashed brightly, as Reggie clumsily moved around.

In the early days after his arrival Reggie the Robot was just starting to learn about himself, the environment and lifestyle he would have to adapt. However, as he became accustomed to his surroundings, and Simon's programming and control skills improved with the help of his older brother, the Robot was starting to impress. Reggie the Robot was definitely getting smarter, thought Buddy and Simon was totally taken and excited by Reggie's growing knowledge and skills. He liked to show him off with glee to his friends and neighbours, but some were less impressed by his new friend, and even made fun of the Robot asking him silly questions like where's your hair?

"Why can't you be quiet when moving around?" asked Simon's pals, who were annoyed especially when playing hide and seek, or other games as Reggie disrupted their fun and always gave the game away, with some strange signal bleep or clumsy squeak, as he sought out Simon or wanted to tag along, while they all played and had fun.

At such times they mocked and made fun of Reggie by calling him funny names like parrot, or saying "you're just a machine trying hard to be human and getting it all wrong!"

But Reggie the Robot would respond to their barbs, saying, "Yes, but a very clever parrot." Or, "you guys make the mistakes and I know how to fix them, even though I'm only a toy robot."

"When I meet a very clever person who can figure out how I work and even if disruptive at first, we can achieve lots of amazing things together.

In fact, we robots are so clever we are starting to work faster, more efficiently than you humans, as our brains are a million times more powerful. We are disrupting and changing existing systems and processes of work globally and our power is increasing with each passing year, so there!" said Reggie.

"There are many examples all around the world right now to prove just how powerful robots really are; in the manufacture of cars, performing surgical operations in hospital, in the kitchen to cook and clean up, in stores to inform and assist customers. We are now being designed to help in crisis situations that are too dangerous for humans, and in space exploration. Robots are being developed in countries like Japan and China to fill jobs where there is a shortage of younger skilled workers. Can you imagine just how much more we robots will achieve in the future," said Reggie. Simon's pals looked at one another and one ventured. "He's right you know! My Uncle Benny's engineering job is now being performed by a robot in Asia."

"See," said Simon – "I told you Reggie was smart and hopefully will eventually be able to do all or most of my chores which would be total bliss."

"In fact, you may be able to tidy and clean my room and put everything in the correct compartment so I can find what I want instantly. And then take out the garbage and that would be perfect," sighed Simon.

"Meaning you will get lazy," said Adrianna – "no, it means I would have more time for practice in my room, knowing it was clean and tidy with more available space," said Simon.

Initially, Buddy sniffed around him and tried to be friends, but the Robot just ignored his presence, Bow barked and Perry remained anxiously in the background.
The three friends gave up trying to figure Reggie out, as he was too unpredictable and erratic, so they mostly avoided him and observed him from a distance.

One thing was very clear though; Simon was totally impressed and excited by his Robot friend, and what they could achieve together. At such times Buddy, Bow and Perry ceased to exist.

Adrianna and her pals did not feel the same way and still adored the three friends. There were lots of friendly and unfriendly neighbours around too who were similar. Even though all kept a noticeable distance from Reggie and appeared only when the robot had retreated, or was out of sight.

Reggie the Robot spent downtime in a remote-controlled hut. Here his batteries were charged and programming occurred.

Simon was still studying robotic programmes to understand how to adapt Reggie's capabilities and skills to his world and lifestyle, with the help of his computer science older brother and his Saturday coding class.

Buddy still couldn't compare the robot to anything in his universe. But even if life was disrupted at times by the arrival of Reggie the Robot, it was not destroyed. In fact, we are very lucky with our world of adventures, discovery and dreams, thought Buddy.

Once, Reggie the robot appeared all-energetic, but that's not all, he started to play music and dance to the tune with multi-coloured lights flashing in every direction.

This time, he took up the whole back yard with the friends racing every which way and from corner to corner, as sparks were flying off the stone surface as Reggie tried to dance around.

Simon raced over – "Reggie, Reggie what's going on?" The three friends stared from the wall in the meadow as the robot tried to break dance.

Buddy then saw Simon race over to the robot's metal box and clicked some switches, this slowed the robot down. Simon then returned with what looked like a remote control and pointed it at Reggie. This stopped the music and Reggie became zombie like as he went into slow motion, as if swimming.

The three friends transfixed, continued to stare at events. Simon then pointed the remote at the robot again and the usual lights started to flash, this time from his chest as Simon guided him back to his house. Reggie the Robot sat in what Simon called the control-resting chair. You could see him through the front glass panel window. Simon told

Adrianna he put the wrong programme in by accident and that break-dancing was the end result.

The only other time the robot went off course was when he imagined he was a soldier or officer commanding his troops in battle. Reggie then just appeared more formal, the lights were darker and the clinks louder as he started marching and shouting orders at his battalion as if in a parade before battle.

The friends retreated to a distant vantage point in the meadow until the robot returned to form and Simon re-engaged him to perform another task. This time it was to help clear the waste shrubbery from the green area off the garden so he and his friends could practice their football skills. As Simon and the robot got busy, the friends slowly gathered around to observe.

Perry, it seemed was beginning to like Reggie and was intrigued by his move, especially during the break dance routine and how the robot was suddenly transformed into a different almost awesome presence, with multi-coloured flashing lights and music in motion. Perry was definitely impressed by such moves if only for a fleeting moment.

Bow on the other hand was at times still spooked and didn't trust any move made by Reggie – whether the clink clank noise as he moved around or the fancy break dance display.

Buddy was ignored so many times and almost trampled on when he tried to get close and befriend Reggie that he just gave up trying, unlike

Simon who appeared at times in awe and enthusiastic when engaging with Reggie.

The three friends were resigned to Reggie the Robot's presence, with his accompanying irritations and disruptions. They now realised Reggie the Robot was a different species they would never come close to understanding.
Just like they could never understand Simon's awe and excitement, even when the robot disrupted events as he did on so many occasions or went the wrong way.

Like when he ventured into the house while Simon was in the garden finishing the lawn. The robot went through the dining room, when suddenly, the table cloth caught in one of the metal spikes protruding from his forearm, pulling the whole dinner set down on the floor to the horror of Simon's mummy.

At this point, the three friends had gathered around silently staring at the robot, knowing he just got into big trouble. "Reggie, you have just shattered the possibility of ever being able to clean my room all by yourself," said Simon.

Simon's pals laughed when he told them the story, one pal then said, "not only did his uncle lose his job in Asia to a robot, but his retired neighbour had a robot do the vacuuming and other household chores as well as helping her to get around." "I told you," said Simon, – "hopefully now you can see what Reggie and those more advanced older robots can achieve."

"In the mean time, there are plenty other interesting and boring tasks Reggie can help with starting with my mathematics exercise," said Simon. "Maybe he will even teach you how to dance laughed another pal."

"You guys are getting weird," said Simon, "Realise, Reggie has the ability to outsmart everyone and it's not even a question of when. "As the world of Robots is expanding rapidly, and they are helping humans operate more efficiently in so many different ways, every day.

6

REGGIE THE ROBOT
AND HIS GLOBAL COMPANIONS
AT WORK

"Even though there's only me around," said Reggie one day, as he bumped into the three friends with Simon. "I am connected to many global robot friends you know. We were designed to perform specific tasks and were all friends before being separated.

They are now making a real difference in so many different areas especially in
the world of work because of their ability to think quicker, learn faster, work smarter thereby performing tasks more efficiently than humans, disrupting old systems and processes with their presence, skills and ever increasing capabilities.

Many in fact have become humanlike helping young and old alike. I can think of a couple of my closest friends who are doing some amazing things to help make life better for everyone.

Even little children can learn from us and start to understand how we function. We can also help them to learn lots of interesting things, even during playtime," said Reggie.

"My friend Willard makes a wonderful family household companion in Japan. He can vacuum, wash up and his more clever friends can even cook meals and play music. His cousin has been designed to work as a butler to assist with household tasks and security.

A couple of miles away his friend Kiera helps an older couple with household chores, programmes the digibox, knows exactly the right temperature to store the wine, does the laundry and some gardening chores like watering the flowers and gathering up the leaves. Ronnie delivers pizzas in the nearby city for a global company.

Then Revels and Rolls work with others in a huge car manufacturing plant. They can work ten times faster than you humans. This reduces the total time taken to make new cars in half, so the new cars get to market earlier.

"But not everyone is as pleased by such developments," said Reggie. "How's that?" asked Simon. "Well, as we Robots become more efficient, there are less jobs for you humans, unless you re-train to learn new skills and that's the key reason we are disliked," said Reggie.

"At the moment, one robot can perform the work of dozens of workers. This saves even more money for the company in wages, as those employees are no longer required for routine positions.

Then there is my other robot friend Pebo at the department store, who greets all the customers and where possible communicates in their native language to answer queries, and give directions so customers can find the required items in the store. Pebo is smart enough to convert currency using the exact exchange rates and she can assist security, thereby reducing theft. Pebo also gets front row to seasonal fashion events, gives press briefings and gets to wear the latest in-season popular clothing labels and accessories.

Other robot folk are increasing in numbers and efficiency too, working in warehouses to manage merchandise, move goods and prepare customers online orders for shipment globally.

Merry has the most fun job of all as she gets to work with children in school, play games, answer questions, help with their tables, spelling and reading classes. Merry makes sad children happy and uninterested children enthusiastic about schoolwork again. After class, lesson summaries are posted to the parent's inbox.

And of course, there are juniors too in our robot family who play with little children at home. They can sing different songs; say their ABCs and numbers, tell nursery rhymes, some can even play musical tunes and dance.

Her other robot friends do more complex tasks in hospitals performing surgery and in other areas of patient care.

Some work at the airport, in hotels checking guests in, and provide information about the services available.

We are starting to arrive in different shapes and sizes too depending on our function," said Reggie.

We hear of other robot folks being deployed to fix dangerous broken power grids and cables, some are even being sent to assist astronauts with space exploration and related projects to discover new planets in our universe. Those are the guys I am most excited about hearing more from when meet. Others help with Deep Ocean projects and are employed by navy and military personnel to assist with complex salvage operations and dangerous combat missions in hostile territories," said Reggie.

"And then there's the smart 'city slickers' robot types, who perform complex financial transactions and advise very rich individuals on best investment and money-making strategies, while others on the team can analyse and produce complex economic data more accurately, ensuring correct decisions are made by business executives. Revells said they are always very serious, focused and in a hurry, but compete fiercely among themselves to win the deal or provide the most rewarding business investment scenario.

Many countries are developing powerful robot models for so many different situations and some are even joining the police, military and conducting musical orchestras.

There are annual competitions and games, which are equivalent to the Olympics for humans, to find the fastest, smartest, skilled and most efficient robots.

Brettles another friend in the US said some of these guys that compete are like giants, and incredibly powerful. They can change shape to perform tasks in restricted or difficult areas that humans can't access.

Some can now even outsmart humans in board game competitions and paint like the great masters of the Renaissance," said Reggie.

"We must find a way to connect with your robot friends or even check out some movies to see how they work and what is going on in the world of Robotics," said Simon, a comment Perry, Buddy and Bow choose to ignore.

"Two of my best friends Sunny and Shine, are now putting a story together from their work in recycling old phones.

They are trying to create a story from each phone based on its owner's world. But the details are vague as it's another top secret project to understand how we can work and interact more like you humans," said Reggie.

"There are so many of us now, with the capability to work alongside you humans in almost every situation. Don't forget, there are other secret projects where robots are being developed and deployed to perform powerful almost life changing tasks around the world, not just for competitions or exhibitions you know," said Reggie.

As a result, some scientists and innovators are worried about our increasing skills and the danger posed to humanity in the future, by more advanced killer robot types. Warnings bells are sounding as a result, so policy makers are seeking ways to regulate our functions, which is reasonable, given such rapid technological developments, especially in artificial intelligence, virtual reality, augmented and mixed reality.

As our designs, coding and sensors now are much more powerful, with increased intelligence levels that enables us to not just work alongside humans, but predict their moves and actions, interact and communicate in their language more effectively too. In fact, some advanced robot types are getting to speak at conferences. Indeed we may be even recognised as new race in the future, and we Robots are just as excited about such possibilities as you humans, as the future belongs to us both," said Reggie.

7

THE LAKE

In the spring, summer and autumn the meadows, woodlands and marshlands are dotted with flowers. There are daisies, bluebells, buttercups and primroses. Adrianna's friends, relatives and neighbours have an annual summer picnic in the meadow by the lake and sometimes, Buddy, Bow and Perry go along too. Uncle James likes to fish on the lake with his friend Mike who has a boat. They usually catch some trout and sometimes other freshwater fish like carp, beam and in the more recent time, rudd and roach.

The children play catch and then a ball game; suddenly everyone is joining in and having a lot of fun. Buddy barks excitedly as if also wanting to be included.

Afterwards the children change into their swimming costumes and go for a swim in the lake. Adrianna instructed the children to stay close to the lakeshore and said the water was very deep and colder further out. She also reminded the children to obey the water safety rules at all times especially at the lake, because it was much more dangerous than the swimming pool, even when the water was very calm, as there were no lifeguards or safety equipment close by, like at the beach or the swimming pool.

All the children obeyed – some yelped, others laughed and shirked, as the water was cold, so they all mostly paddled and played splash.

Bow and Perry sniffed the grass, ran around, and then lay down with the others. Jane gave them some biscuits, but Buddy the brave and energetic one, as always, quickly swam out past the children, splashing loudly, creating big white waves as he swam towards the long reeds.

Suddenly, two beautiful white swans flew up from the reeds over the lake, skimming the water as they landed close to the trees on the other side of the lake to join others. Startling some migratory diving ducks, that from a distance, looked like the tufted and goldeneye ducks, who disappeared underwater, only to emerge again at another position on the lake, as they fed on the feathery stonewort and other underwater vegetation.

Buddy swam back by the water lilies towards the large rock close to the shore where the children had gathered around. "They are from the mute swan family, as the Whopper and Berwick swans will not arrive here until October from Iceland and Siberia and return home in March," said Mike. However right now, the Swan family were fully alert, and no doubt alarmed by the sudden interruption to their world, as they looked over from the far side of the lake, as if telling everyone they were now out of reach.

As Buddy came out of the water and shook himself dry, the children were pointing across the lake towards the swans that were suddenly joined by small dark cygnets.

Buddy started barking again, dancing around wagging his tail excitedly as the children were trying to count the number of baby swans called cygnets.

First, they counted eight chicks, but then others would appear from underwater and disappear again, as if trying to trick the children.

Adrianna said, there was between eight and ten little ones and some appeared to be either having an underwater swim, or trying to fish.

Similar to the Shell ducks and a couple of Mallards further down the shore and the Dippers who hunt for food underwater. A Grey Heron waited patiently in a sheltered inlet by the reeds, at the edge of the lake for a juicy trout or frogs to emerge. And few more migratory dabbling ducks from the wigeon and teal families were visible, as they fed on some crowfoot flowers and submerged fennel growing along the shallow margins of the lake.

While the may flies, a couple of hover flies, and spread-wing-damsel flies took to the air to avoid afternoon predators. An abundance of stoneflies were visible further out on the lake. According to Mike, a high population of stoneflies indicated unpolluted waters and therefore, a healthy oxygenated environment for fish to breed.

Beyond the lake far in the distance, is the magic mountain. According to an old legend, the mountain got its name from a little princess who was turned into a spring posy by a wicked witch when she refused to give away her puppy Pebbles. Some say the sparkling stones are from the golden rays and sparkling silver that appeared when the witches spell was broken.

According to the story...One day as Theodora, was playing close to the lake with her puppy, a wicked witch flew over the mountain and across the lake on a huge white bird with black eyes and set down by the trees across from where Theodora was playing with Pebbles. The wicked witch came over to Theodora and spoke softly saying she would give Theodora some magic sweets if she would give her puppy away. Theodora then asked if she could taste the sweets first and then she would decide if she wanted to give the puppy.

So, the wicked witch agreed, but warned Theodora if she ate the last one without agreeing to give the puppy away, she would be turned into a flower that would bloom only in springtime.
She would remain a flower unless the magic spell was broken and this would only be only possible, if someone picked a bunch of spring poesies and scented their sweet smelling petals indoors at a party gathering, or if the rainbow started or ended, where she was growing.

Theodora ate a magic sweet and it tasted delicious, she settled on the grass at the edge of the lake among the flowering posies.
One sweet tasted more delicious than the last. "Thank you old lady – I've never tasted such delicious sweets. Even Father never brings such amazing treats," said Theodora.

So, Theodora continued munching and was starting to feel drowsy, almost forgetting her puppy and the fact that she should not eat the last sweet in the packet. But after she ate the last yellow and green coloured sweet, there was a loud hissing wind, dark clouds hung over head and Theodora started to feel cold.

"Oh dear, I must hurry back, I haven't got my rain coat," said Theodora. As she stood up, after eating the last sweet, the wicked witch appeared with Pebbles in her arms, and said "young lady I'm taking your puppy," said the wicked witch. "No, you are not," cried Theodora, "Pebbles is mine, besides, Father won't let you have him." So the wicked witch then cast the magic spell and Theodora instantly became a spring posy.

So when Theodora did not return home that evening, a search party was sent out; Many days, nights, weeks, months and years went by and everyone was distraught as no trace of Theodora could be found no matter how hard they searched.

The Earl Alfred and his wife Heather were bereft and were given to an unending sadness. They didn't know what to do or where to turn for help and everyone was distraught. How they loved and now missed their little princess.

Some said Theodora drowned in the lake, others said she was taken by the gypsies, more said she got kidnapped by pirates who sometimes would explore the lake when sailing the ocean close by.

But nobody knew what happened to Theodora. Everyone in the kingdom was very sad at the mention of her name, as they remembered the sweet princess in the beautiful dress with golden curls, just eight years old, so young, if captured by strangers... Prayers were said every day and candles lit for her safe return, in the jewel encrusted stone chapel that her Father had built.

Still no trace could be found no matter how many searched. After a weary ten years, the Earl and his wife grew tired, his wife became ill, and so they decided to return to their residence in the warmer climate of the South of France.

All was agreed, they would sail in the spring, but decided to have some parties before leaving, and Theodora always had a birthday party in spring.

That drew instant tears from everyone at Theodora's mention. "You're right," said his wife Heather, "because her birthday was in spring, we always gathered glorious spring flowers and put them all round the house. And we continued to do this throughout summer and autumn when there were flowers and beautiful berries on the branches in the garden, woodland and meadows."

"Well this spring time will not pass without us picking all kinds of posies from the meadow, woodland, marshlands and of course the garden," said Alfred the Earl. "It's bound to lift our spirits and let Theodora know that we haven't forgotten her."

"We will gather the posies for the party celebrations next week; it's the last party before we leave for France, so let's make it special to remind us of our little, lost princess" sobbed the Earl. "I will get larger vases ready for the spring posies," said Mabel the housekeeper. "Make sure there is an especially beautiful arrangement in the entrance hall," instructed Heather, the Earls wife.

There was lots of activity as everyone prepared for the final party. The best meats of the day were on offer, like wild boar, deer, rabbit and selection of wild fowl in season. Along with fish from the local river and lake, like mackerel, trout and salmon were all prepared for the huge banquet.

Traditional drinks made from hops, barley and others from berries were on offer, along a variety of liquor from travels overseas and earlier voyages of friends to discover new worlds in faraway lands.

This party was smaller than the usual, but was a lavish affair with mostly family, close friends and neighbours. As young and old started to gather in the great hall, there was a buzz of excitement all around. Some cousins arrived, friends followed them and then a young man arrived with a present for the Earl. The housekeeper went to find the Earl while the young man waited by the sideboard in the entrance hall. The Earl then arrived very happy to see Prince Rupert, sent with a gift by his father the High King, who was unwell and unable to attend.

"Oh," said the excited Earl, "tell his Majesty your father that I am delighted to receive his most gracious and generous gift. Any idea what's in the box, or should it remain a surprise," asked the Earl.

"It's Fathers best vintage I can tell you that. The red is woody with a fruity aroma, and the white is a taste of sweet summer berries with an uplifting aroma of flowering posies. Actually, similar to this refreshing selection and at the same moment, the Prince reached for a few spring posies and scented their sweet smelling petals.

Suddenly, the huge crystal vase full of spring posies tumbled off the sideboard onto the ground, to the absolute shock of the young prince and the Earl who was standing alongside. Next moment a whirl of grey cloud arose from the ground followed by golden rays sparkling over a huge burst of mist.

 The golden rays continued to fill the room before disappearing through the front door. The young man grew pale, as he could not understand what was happening. The light golden rays with silver sparkle were seen from the hall. People thought this was a party display, and started to come towards the front hall.

Suddenly the most beautiful girl emerged, with blond curls..."Father," said the little girl. With that the Earl turned pale. "Theodora...darling, my little darling...his voice shaking is it really you?" And the little girl replied, "yes Father, it is I." The Earl was so over come with joy, uttering ...your mother... Suddenly shocked...with the sounds of amazement and then silence, her mother made her way to the reception room, "what...Theodora, ...It can't be...Theodora darling." ..."It is mother," said Theodora. With that the mother fainted. ...Her father, rushed over to hug her in a tearful embrace. They all then gathered round the Earl's wife Heather, who was tended to and brought to recover in the lounge overlooking the garden..."We were all so very worried and never did want to give up hope of seeing you again," said

Kingsley the Butler. "Where have you been darling – do tell us what happened Theodora," pleaded her overjoyed father.

Everybody then gathered round to see and hear Theodora recount the story of how and why she disappeared for so long. "That time by the lake, a wicked witch came by ...I remember now...she wanted my puppy Pebbles and offered me some sweets.
The witch said not to eat the last one, without giving her Pebbles my puppy...So I tasted the sweets and they were so delicious. Soon I felt very sleepy and must have forgotten her instructions, and eat the last sweet," recounted Theodora.

"So, the wicked witch cast a spell turning me into spring posy. And said the magic spell would not be broken and I would most likely remain a spring poise forever, unless the poesies were picked, placed in a vase, and their petals were scented indoors at a party gathering, or if the rainbow started or ended where I was growing, but this never happened.

"And I was just telling your father how the special vintage drinks in the box tasted like the sweet aroma of berries and spring posies combined – almost like a spring floral bouquet with barley and berries, but slightly stronger, with an intoxicating effect," said Prince Rupert, a tall handsome blond haired young man.

"And at that moment I just took a few posies smelled the petals while comparing them to fathers vintage wine," said Rupert. "Young man," said the Earl, standing shakily and gripping the sideboard at the same time - "we owe you our life, Theodora was our life, we lost her and now because of you we've found her again," said the Earl. "How is your father, the High King and Clan"? He was poorly, but improved after the fall, and is home now resting, wishing he could be here today, but sent this gift to you instead," replied Rupert."

"You are the man of the moment," said the Earl...Theodora, darling, how wonderful and lucky we are to have found you again darling," said her father, the Earl. "Papa, can I get dressed for the party," "of course my darling." "Oh dear, what will you wear, we don't have any clothes to fit you now," said her mother.

"In that case, I will go as I am, besides, I don't want to miss a minute of the party," said Theodora. Just then her best friends Kitty, Christina and Alice rushed in ..."there she is," said Kitty ..."Theodora, oh my god...it is true, we just heard they found you," said an animated Alice. "We were so worried, and sad when no trace could be found, no matter how hard we searched -where have you been all this time," asked Alice. And with that, they all rushed over to hug Theodora. "We thought we would never see you again," said Christina..."you look the same," said Kitty. "You're taller," said a shocked Alice.

"We have so much to tell you," gushed Kitty. "Ah girls, good to see you," said The Earl, can you help Theodora find a dress for the party as she has outgrown all her old clothes."

"Theodora...can wear my new yellow and green dress Mildred just made with a linen and silk surcoat," said an animated Kitty. "I think you will prefer my cream and gold dress with a crimson over layer, as its bright and a perfect party dress," said Alice - I will go back home and bring it here for you to try it on." "And I have crimson and cream slippers that will be perfect and great for dancing," suggested Christina. "Oh that's wonderful, I am so very happy now to see you all again," said Theodora.

"My poor darling, how dreadful it was to have lost you and how terrible it must have been for you. Do tell us what happened Theodora," said her father.

"Well I did I did miss you all very much in the early days were terrible," said Theodora, "as I was stuck with just flowering posies, grasses and the little animal, birds, bees and insects that live among them. But it became easier and more interesting as time went on. I hibernated in winter, waking up in early spring to the sound of the songbirds, as they hurried about building their nests.

The blackbirds were the earliest risers and started singing at dawn followed by the thrush and sparrow. The blackbirds were the bossy ones who defended their territory and hated intruders. The wrens and robins joined the other songbirds in sweet chorus. The sparrows are definitely the most adaptable to humans and found in large numbers in villages and communities around the world.

The robin's bright red breast also served as a warning to other birds to keep their distance as they protected their territory. Still, everyone liked the robin family, as they were around all year and especially popular at Christmas time. They blended in with the wrens, sparrows, thrushes and wagtail - all singing sweetly in springtime, especially when want to attract a mate or defend their territory.

In ancient mythology, the wrens were king of the year until an ancient pagan ritual saw them killed on the 26th of December and the subsequent cry "help to bury the wren" on Stephens Day by the Wren Boys. The robin family replaced the wrens after this time. They are the tamest songbirds too and get closest to humans, as they hop around inquisitively on tree branches and window ledges, oftentimes searching for food especially during the colder winter months. The robin sings the sweetest and longest of all the birds. In ancient folklore, it is said that the robin was given this special gift, after helping Mary and Joseph into Egypt.

The cuckoo calling each evening signalled the arrival of spring. Still the cuckoo was disliked by other birds, as she never built her own nest, but moved into the nests of other birds, laid her eggs and left it to others to take care of her young, until they migrated.

The songbirds got to work building their nests, which were mostly neat and small, hidden away from view in the trees.

The larger birds from the crow family, like the magpies, jays, rooks, jackdaws, hooded crows and their visiting European cousins were also busy at work. Their nests were larger and made from twigs high up in the tall trees, but always looked messy.

The crows and magpies worked hard all spring building their nests while keeping a noticeable distance from each other. As almost everyone disliked the magpies and blamed them for stealing their eggs, making them unpopular friends and unwelcome guests.

I will never forget one springtime just as we posies arrived and started to bloom in the usual patches around the woodland. "We sensed something wasn't quite right. The willow tree continued to weep and the crow family were huddled together in conference," said Theodora.

"We soon discovered that their woodland world was disturbed by woodcutters who had chopped down some of large old oak trees to make furniture, shoes and leather goods. Some beech and hazel trees also disappeared, leaving the nearby willow trees forlorn, but were pleased their bark and sap wasn't cut to extract the medicinal salicin, that was used to make asprin.

There was such commotion among the crow family for days especially the hooded crows, rooks and magpies, as their favourite nesting place in the tall trees had disappeared, and were bickering as to who would take the nearby sycamore trees, with the magpies winning there.

Their cousins, the jackdaws, were organised and loyal and nested alone in holes in craggy cliffs, suggested some join them in the nearby hills and mountains, as it was a safe nesting place and there was also a clear view all around from the cliffs and mountaintops.

The Jays, invited others to join them in the grassy areas and sand dunes, but neither locations appeared suitable for the rooks or hooded crows.

The rooks were then suddenly cheerful when they found some huge horse chestnut trees and some promising tall coniferous trees further along that might be suitable, with their constant green foliage to provide extra safety for nesting.

Two senior hooded crows followed the advice of their European cousins, who said the coniferous pine trees were cut down more frequently by woodcutters, for their superior quality wood and therefore would make a dangerous nesting location. So the hooded crows opted instead to join the raptors in the huge old horse chestnut trees.

The birds of prey like the falcon, sparrow hawk, hen harrier and kestrel were unpredictable, sharp and fast in the air and on the ground, especially when hunting for food. These birds of prey lived off little animals like birds, mice and frogs; they were also unfriendly and worse still, competed to catch the juiciest food.

The falcons were confident and very fast birds in flight whose prey hardly ever escaped and they scared everyone.

The sparrow hawks were smaller birds of prey with very strong claws that tore the flesh off its prey.

The hen harriers were viewed as the smarter birds of prey because they flew close to the ground, while circling their prey at the same time, which usually was small rabbits, mice, frogs or other unsuspecting folk, including some birds.

The kestrels took the opposite approach, and flew higher due to their strong wings and superior vision, dropping at lightning speed on their prey.

The game birds like the grouse, pheasant and wild ducks were nervous birds, probably because they were hunted, killed and cooked for their tender, tasty meat, and their colourful feathers were often used as a decoration in millinery. We were often woken up or alerted to intruders, by their sudden flight from the long grasses, as they were noisy birds when disturbed, and created a huge racket as they flew quickly from their resting place.

As we posies started to bloom in early springtime, the lambs danced and played, especially on sunny days, in the now enclosed fields of pastureland and on the hills in the distance.

The hares moved from the woodland to the pastureland and played with their young, who are known as leverets. They lived in a flat grassy sheltered patch called forms instead of a warren, and only emerged at dawn or dusk," said Theodora.

In springtime, farmers were busy sowing the crops, others were planting trees and hedging and draining the land to release excess water to improve land quality.

I overheard some folk complaining about you papa and your plans to extend the deer park, enclose the orchard and build a high wall around the demesne, blocking access to the river and the plentiful supply of salmon and trout. This seemed to annoy and disappoint everyone.

We spring posies had a shorter time in bloom than the daisies, who had so many stories to tell us from the previous summer and autumn seasons, of folks who picnicked or fished by the lake on lazy summer days, and of others who hunted on foot and on horseback in search of the hare, cleaver fox or deer.

We also saw folks returning from a voyage in far-away lands, solders in uniform marching to battle and pilgrims on their journey to holy places of retreat and worship" said Theodora.

"The gorse or whin, as it is also known and blackthorn trees were the first to blossom in springtime, along with beautiful colourful flowers like the snowdrops, bluebells, daisies and my family of spring posies would all bloom in the warmer spring and summer sunshine.

There were competitions to select the tallest, most beautiful and sweetest scenting posies. Would it be the bluebells who nestled by the trees, the delicate and demure snowdrops or my family of primroses that grew in sheltered patches of pasturelands and woodlands?

The daisies competed fiercely with the buttercups that grew all around the meadows and woodlands, coming into bloom just as we were going back to sleep.

The buttercups argued that they were the most popular flower of all, as they were a bright sunny colour and strong even when trod on by the cunning fox, hare, badger, bunny rabbits and deer, as they still survived and bloomed all summer long.
And were also favoured by the honeybee and bumblebee communities, along with the red admiral and peacock butterflies, who stopped by almost every day to rest on their sunny yellow petals.

The white and pink clover thought they were superior and boasted of their medicinal powers, abundance of nectar and their ability to nourish and improve the soil, so everyone grew healthy and strong each year. My family of spring posies insisted they were special because they had useful medicinal properties in helping to heal wounds and act as a sedative.

My neighbours, the bluebells suggested they were the prettiest flowers of spring and were also useful, as their bulbs underground contained a sap that was used as glue for bookbinding. They were pestered, especially by the bumblebees who appeared to love their sweet smelling petals. The worker bees descended with urgency early in the morning to collect the nectar and pollen and continued throughout the day as they built huge stores of honey for winter hibernation.

The honeybees were busy too collecting pollen and nectar for their winter honey store, even though they didn't hibernate during cold, damp and rainy winter months.

So it wasn't so bad after all," said Theodora, "and as the years passed by so very quickly, I started to forget about my friends, Kitty, Alice and Christina, the tea parties and birthday parties, even Pebbles, but not you or papa or mama.

"And we went to the chapel every day to pray and light candles of hope, for your safe return," said the Earl.

"Well your prayers and good wishes kept me safe and out of harm's way, because the wicked witch did return to find me, on the huge big bird - this time with her cat. I heard her say to her cat Ferris "we have not had any luck since that puppy arrived; perhaps I shouldn't have taken him".

Then the wicked witch said to the huge cat resting on her shoulder. "Ferris my furry and fearless friend who sees all things, find the spring posy I cast my magic spell over." The witch stroked the cat, who appeared to scan the ground from his perch on her shoulder, before pouncing down into the long grass, and that was a scary moment. "As I thought her cat Ferris would discover who and where I was growing, as he prowled cautiously though the long grasses and posies, examining each one with his exceptionally big eyes," recounted Theodora.

"The cat then got distracted by a large frog that leaped through the grass and had a lucky escape, in part because of its ability to change colour as a camouflage in order to adapt to its environment. It is said, that in olden times, folks could predict the weather by the colour of the frog's underbelly. The frogs I realised had the best of both worlds," said Theodora, "living on land during the warm summer, tending to their young and then hibernating in winter at the bottom of the stream or shallow part of the lake. "At the same time, a large pheasant noisily flew up from a clump of tall grasses and rushes, startling Ferris the cat, who now appeared forlorn, moved slowly as if searching for the next prey, while the wicked witch continued to plead in a shaky voice."

"Ferris my furry and fearless friend, who sees all things, find the spring posy I cast my magic spell over, so we can take her back and maybe our good luck, peace and happiness will return, as that puppy has just been trouble."

"If I could find the little girl, and take her back with me perhaps things would change," said the witch, as she called out again, "Theodora, Theodora, where are you darling, I want to break the magic spell, so you can return." And this cajoling went on for a while, promising various tempting treats, sweetly saying, "look Theodora, I have your favourite magic sweets, and this time, they will break the spell. Or I live in a magic kingdom where you can have anything you want and the land of chocolate is close by."

"But I was not going to be fooled this time," said Theodora. "I was terrified and stayed very quiet, hoping she wouldn't discover who I was or where I was growing.

The blue bells whispered, "are you sure Theodora," and the snowdrops ventured "but why Theodora – remember the early days, how you hated being a spring posy? Would you not like the chance of a better more exciting time with the witch"? I said "absolutely not after what she done to my adorable puppy Pebbles and me," said Theodora.

"The wicked witch was then almost blinded by the bright mid-day sun that sparkled across the lake, as she placed her hands over her eyes and covered her head with the hood of her cloak. I was so delighted and relieved when she called out to the cat, "Ferris, Ferris we will retreat and return." With that, the cat leaped onto the witches shoulder again and she almost collapsed, before crawling back on the big bird, shouting "away Dust Lightening, let us speed away."

"I always hoped the magic spell would be broken, and one day you would find me, and you did thanks to Rupert," said Theodora. "We are all so thrilled," said the Earl's wife, with tears streaming down her face, "with so many days without your darling...everyone we knew prayed and hoped for such a day."

"What a marvellous surprise...Let the celebrations begin," said her father the Earl. The entire kingdom and every kingdom beyond celebrated. Trumpets, horns, and drums sounded, lutes and harps played the sweetest music, lullabies were sung, jesters performed and the laughter and merry making continued late into the night. The day Theodora's magic spell was broken was celebrated every year thereafter, making spring the happiest season of the year for everyone in the Kingdom and beyond. That day, the sparkling golden rays continued to float into the air, before descending on the mountain.

According to ancient folklore this why the mountain appears to still sparkle in the bright sunshine, as if diamonds were hiding or embedded in the stones and rocks that peer up around the flora and fauna covering the mountain.

"We will definitely have to go on a hike to explore the mountain one time," suggested Mike. "I agree," said Adrianna "but the magic mountain is an adventure for another day, as it's a three hour walk and over an hour's drive from the lake."

"The older boys in the scouts went there last summer to explore and gather some sample rocks for their geography project, but I don't think they found any diamonds in the stones, or maybe they didn't look hard enough," said Mike.

"We could have our picnic there next year maybe even find some stones with jewels or diamonds as they sparkle in the sun, but don't forget, the mountain sparkles even more brightly in the snow, in fact it truly is a magic mountain in the snow," said Adrianna.

"Maybe we should take an Archaeology class to develop our knowledge of how to identify hidden objects of ancient treasure, symbolic stone carvings from Celtic times or rock formations from the ice age. This would make the trip more interesting next time," said Mike.

"Good idea, as a trip to the mountain would definitely make fun adventure next year when my cousins are here on vacation, as they love nature and the natural environment," said Adrianna.

"Actually mountains were sacred symbols at home and abroad for Christians in ancient times. Moses received the Ten Commandments from God when on Mount Sinai," said Mike. "Very true - just like our own holy mountain is a place where pilgrims journey to annually and on reaching the summit, worship and rest for their return journey home. Folks who enjoy the great outdoors also climb the mountain and the others close by for recreation or a sporting challenge, and the opportunity to enjoy the views across the ocean to the islands beyond on a clear sunny day," said Adrianna.

8

A TRIP TO TOWN

Adrianna often took Buddy and Perry to town. Bow always stayed home as he would not get into the car and missed out on another interesting adventure. Adrianna would take them with her as she shopped. Perry and Buddy were always content just to stay by her side on their lead and observe as they followed along. Other times when in a hurry, she would leave them in the car and from there they would peer out the window observing all that was going on.

Perry and Buddy enjoyed their trip to town and gave the impression they found it more interesting than the countryside. There was so much going on, people shopping or just walking by, some were riding their bikes, others laughing and talking or having coffee by the café window or outdoors.

Folks walking their puppies or big dogs - Buddy then noticed one tall man going by speaking on this mobile and raising his hand to acquaintances as he strolled along with three puppies on their lead. The puppies were all the same white and brown colour and slightly smaller and shorter than Perry.

One yelped and the others then looked backed as the man continued talking on his phone, tugging the three along at the same time.

He was like the man in the picture on Adrianna's wall, which is why Buddy probably noticed him, but with a different coloured hat.

If only Bow was adventurous enough and came to town too there would be three of us, thought Buddy, but as the man disappeared into the crowd in the busy street, Buddy decided his three puppies were too small and would never make suitable playmates for Perry, Bow and himself. It is very unlikely they would ever adjust to quieter life in the country and the rough and tumble of the great outdoors. Or even have any interest in exploring the meadows and woodlands that he Bow and Perry called home, after the bustle and constant movement of the crowded town.

And Felix the cat wasn't quite right either, thought Buddy, as he played unfairly too, even sometimes cheated, using his sharp claws to try and win. And when he started to lose the game, would swiftly escape over the nearby wall, wagging his tail in a superior gesture, as he looked back from a safe vantage point, leaving the three friends defeated and humiliated every time.
Still, Buddy liked the countryside and woodlands as adventure and fun were never far away in the lush green meadows and woodlands. And thank God for Sandy, Mrs Mallery's puppy, who played with the three friends, each time they went to visit with Adrianna.

Then there was Otes the small black puppy, who would race with Perry in the pasture close by and this was the one time Perry always won. Buddy liked Otes as he was always happy and played fairly, even if it was only for occasional short bursts of fun every once in a while, before retreating with urgency home.

There was always something new to discover or some strange occurrences to contend with in the meadows and woodlands thought Buddy.

With cunning fox, the speedy rabbit, the touchy Mrs Moo and Mrs Sheep or Polly and Hunter the ponies, showing off as they raced nearby or trekked around the village.

The friends continued to peer out the window of Adrianna's car hoping she would soon appear but in the meantime, there was plenty going on around town. Children going home from school, some making their way to the big school bus waiting close by. There were trucks, big lorries and different types of cars and jeeps everywhere, all moving slowly by. Everyone was moving in one direction or another and Perry and Buddy desperately wanted to join them.

On this trip to town, Adrianna took both Perry and Buddy shopping. First, they went to the green grocers where Adrianna got some delicious fruit, vegetables and wood for the fire. Then they all went to the bookshop and as Adrianna was leaving she bumped into her friend Ursla who was just after collecting her 5-year-old son James from school. Adrianna and Ursla talked and laughed for a few moments, and as they passed the boutique, Adrianna pointed to a dress in the window, that she thought would be perfect for her friend's wedding. "Why don't you go in and try it on and I will take care of Buddy and Perry," said Ursla. "Do you mind, I will be very quick," said Adrianna.

As Ursla checked her mobile phone James was eating an ice cream and then started to stroke Buddy and Perry, both puppies liked James. Suddenly James started crying, Ursla look at him to see what was wrong, and she saw Buddy had taken James's chocolate ice cream and was eating it while the remainder had dropped onto Jame's uniform. While Ursla was preoccupied with James, Perry raced off.

Just as Adrianna had changed into the dress and shoes in the boutique, and was viewing it in the long mirror, trying to decide with the help of the assistant, whether the frills were a little too flamboyant and made her look more like a flamenco dancer than wedding guest. Then suddenly she heard James crying, along with sudden breaking of cars coming to a standstill. At the same time, she heard Ursla call out, "Perry, Perry, come back." Adrianna hurried to the door and saw Perry racing across the street, with traffic coming to an abrupt stand-still. "Oh Adrianna, I'm sorry," said Ursla. "I better try and catch him," replied Adrianna, as she instantly raced after, calling out, "Perry, Perry come back, wait."

"Callum and JE, Oh my god, it can't be." "Yes it is," said Calum. "Wow, that's a fancy dress, a designer number," said JE. "No I've deliberately downsized," replied Adrianna dismissively. "You're kidding, let me do you up," said JE. "No, I...actually good idea...I didn't have time and I must dash now guys, I have a crisis – I need to catch Perry," said Adrianna. "Can we get a picture," asked JE. "Only if you can catch up," replied Adrianna as she trudged across the street after Perry who was quickly disappearing in the distance.

As she passed some younger children going to or coming from a ball game, she could hear comments like "she needs my skateboard." Followed by giggles and "Last week my snowboard would have worked..."It's true," commented JE smiling. Then he paused and asked their teacher if he could take an informal picture of the group.

At the same time as Adrianna hurried along in pursuit of Perry, passed a group of gaggling girls, she heard utterances of "that's the dress - that's the same dress Sylivian wore to her party"... your right", agreed another. I cannot believe this, can anyone go anywhere or do anything, even in an emergency, and JE is also enjoying the fun run, thought Adrianna.

Perry continued across the cobbled stone surface of the country market and Adrianna was hoping he wouldn't do any damage, as she could hear the sound of bottles clink, after Perry brushed against the display table, with a sign that read, craft beer, wine and juices, as he raced onward in the direction of the river, and was now beyond reach. While Adrianna struggled to catch up, in shoes that were starting to hurt, hopelessly calling out, "Perry, Perry wait, come back."

As she paused to catch a breath, JE and Callum just caught up. "You're as crazy as ever," said Callum.

"Thanks, I know and I realise you are enjoying this fleeting moment, but I must catch ...I need you to try and catch Perry." "The dress is," said JE tailing off ..."ridiculous for such an event, I know, but the dress is not mine, I was just trying it for size." explained a breathless Adrianna. "It's a sunny day and looks perfect," said JE, as he continued to click on his high powered video camera lens, while assuming different posture angles.

"Great shot and the back drop is perfect," said JE. "Who cares about the back drop - Perry is almost in the river," replied a panicked Adrianna.

I can't believe you said that, the backdrop and vista beyond always mattered for you in a picture," replied JE. I agree but not when the foreground is so ridiculously wrong, as in my attire," snapped Adrianna. "Ok ok, but the overall event is perfect in this instance, with maybe a couple of edits," replied a JE. "Sure, whatever," replied breathless Adrianna, relieved Callum had just rescued Perry, before he went for a swim in the river.

"Seriously you guys, I cannot believe meeting you here...but glad I did," said Adrianna smiling. "And your shot is picture perfect for my 'Urban and on the Move' portfolio in contrasting locations," said JE. "Really, how interesting," replied Adrianna dismissively as she took a yelping and panicked sounding Perry by the lead and tried to quite him.

"We have a shot and short story now, as we have captured you with mischievous Perry in a busy but relaxed setting," said JE. A snapshot of the country market. Others going a ball game, and earlier on a bridal party after the wedding ceremony, with the bride and the train of her dress positioned against the stone, under the trees with a river backdrop. Then a mini crisis emerges, as her bouquet falls of the wall into the river. Folks then gather around in their best wedding attire, helpless as they watch the bouquet being swepted along by the current, past three Swans, who look on perplexed.

Folks on the opposite side are fishing and oblivious to events, others are meandering by eating ice cream. So casual and formal, relaxed and in motion, converge to create an interesting cocktail of images that depict our portfolio theme 'Urban and on the Move' in contrasting environments," explained Callum.

"This is one of many locations, as we have already covered four European cities, eight US cities, two in South America and two Canadian cities, in order to compare and contrast composition, style, and lifestyles. Instantaneous shots that depict our 'Urban and on the Move' portfolio in contrasting locations," explained JE. "Sounds great, I can't wait to see the portfolio, the fact that I looked ridiculous as I trooped after Perry in inappropriate shoes and this dress, obviously didn't register," said Adrianna.
No really, you miss the point – your picture was so instantaneous and authentic, it countered the negatives," said JE. "Not sure I like the sound of that," replied Adrianna cautiously.

"I think you will love the finished work," said Callum. "I'm sure I will, as you guys always create inspiring award winning works," replied Adrianna.

"You're not so bad yourself," said JE. "Thanks JE, I love your project concept," said Adrianna.

"It's actually a concept aligned to product, purpose, function, and functionality, that moves and influences the viewer to desire, seek out and ultimately buy your product. I personally like the idea of depicting merchandise in motion or around a story," explained Callum.

"Sounds fascinating, as always the dreamers and innovators, and I must get back with the dress – I guess I'll have to buy it now," said Adrianna. "Why not," said Callum. "It's a perfect fit and suits you," said JE. "Sure sure ... I remember you also liked my hallowed costume that time too," replied Adrianna. "No, I mean yes – you looked funny as opposed to scary, and then you made your lips black". "To match my eyes and nails," said Adrianna. "That was scary and funny, but great," replied JE smiling. "I tried to combine Goth and Vintage style, to create the perfect Halloween fancy dress attire." "And you succeeded, it's just JE doesn't like girls who wear black makeup," said Callum.

"Well who cares – this dress is different and the colours are great for a late spring summer wedding," agreed Adrianna. "Absolutely," agreed Callum.

Just then, Ursla emerged with Buddy and James. "There you are Adrianna, I'm so so sorry Adrianna, it's just Buddy started to eat James ice cream as he patted him, and half the ice cream cone fell on to his school uniform and as I tried to wipe it off, Perry slipped away," explained Ursla. "You don't need to explain Ursla, its Perry, he is always so impulsive," said Adrianna. ..."The dress," said Ursla in amusement..."I know...I know, I should have changed back first," replied Adrianna. "I spoke to them in the boutique - they are actually amused, joking how it's a creative way to showcase their dress, and they have your things," said Ursla. "Great, - oh I'm sorry," said Adrianna, meet Callum and JE, old friends from art school."

"This is Ursla my friend and her son James." "Nice to meet you," said Ursla," and all exchanged greetings.

James was then starting to get impatient, and was asking Ursla "when will you buy me another ice cream Mommy." "We will get another one soon, but first Adrianna has to go back, change, buy her dress and put Perry and Buddy in the car and we will then get another ice cream.

"Great to see you guys," said Adrianna as she reach out to hug both. "We have to go and I desperately need to lose these shoes, but let's catch up one time." "Absolutely Adrianna – let's get together when the portfolio is complete," said Callum. "Great idea, see you then," said Adrianna as she hugged both again and waved good-bye.

She then realized Perry once again managed to slip away. I cannot believe Perry, he's escaped again," said a panicked Adrianna. "I thought he was with you," replied Ursla. "He was and just for a second I forgot," said Adrianna.

She could see Perry running onwards through the gardens and picnic area, past the outdoor shop, restaurant, beauty salon and bakery, towards the boy and girl sitting outside the café by the square with another poodle. Thankfully, a traffic warden managed to grab Perry's lead, as he tried to cross over at the top of the street.

Adrianna could then hear a loud siren, and cars started to slow down and pull over, as a police patrol motorcycle went by moving slowly through the traffic followed closely by the Emergency Ambulance as they made their way onwards towards the square at the end of the street.

Then Callum and JE passed by in a large four-wheel drive and almost pulled over but were unable to do so, on seeing a red-faced Adrianna on a second rescue mission.

Thank God there was another distraction to disrupt the traffic flow thought Adrianna, as she hurried towards the traffic warden who was clutching Perry.

"Thank you so much," said Adrianna as she took Perry who at this point was panting and flustered. Adrianna was also red faced and embarrassed, "I am awfully grateful to you Sir for capturing Perry and stopping him from causing any further disruption today," said Adrianna.

"First and second responders together," said the traffic warden smiling, alluding to the more serious emergency service just gone by, and his rescue and recovery act in catching Perry.

"Was there an accident," inquired Adrianna, as she held Perry. "I heard some visitor holidaying in the area became unwell and that's all I know.

Let's hope he or she will be ok and it's not too serious," replied Adrianna, "I hope so," said the traffic warden. "Keep a close eye on that little rascal won't you miss – I must get back to work now."

"Thank you again Sir for your help in catching Perry, he is such a naughty fellow and so restless today."
Ursla, James and Buddy just caught up after following along in the background, anxiously observing events. "How such a little fellow, who is always timid and cuddly, could also be so very naughty is puzzling," said Ursla.

"'Double trouble' just describes our day so far," said Adrianna, after the Buddy incident followed closely by Perry's escape escapades. "Your right," replied Ursla. "I know Perry is impulsive, but I have no idea why he is so restless today," said Adrianna.
James then started whinging, tugging on Ursla's sleeve about wanting another ice cream after Buddy eat his one.

"Right, we will get you another ice cream and I know the best place," said Adrianna. Its fine really – James is just being difficult and you need to return to the boutique," said Ursla.
"I insist – let's get in my car it will be quicker – the car is parked just over the way by the pizza restaurant," said Adrianna. First stop, the boutique to change back and buy the dress.

"I can then park close to the ice cream shop and after I need to go to the chocolate shop to buy some sweet treats for tea. Emily and Beth are coming to visit and you are welcome to join us," said Adrianna.

"I would love to, but another time," replied Ursla. "Do you remember last time, Perry and Buddy came with us, as we walked through the demesne of country estate to do some sailing, and Melissa was giving us a history lesson from her school project on the planning, Georgian design and architecture of the town, as we walked by the river," recounted Ursla.

"I do remember," said Adrianna, "as James fed the scattering of Shell ducks, some Guillemot gulls also decided to join the feast.

Buddy jumped into the water followed by Perry the poodle, forcing the ducks to flee in every direction - leaving a pool of muddy water that submerged the treats.
When Buddy got out of the water, he shook himself dry, splashing the muddy water onto James's school uniform and your shoes. And when Perry emerged, he was grey instead of snow white. "Well that will not happen now or anytime soon, as Perry and Buddy are both grounded for being so naughty today," said Adrianna.

Finally, the friends bid their farewell and went their separate ways. How the day had slipped by so quickly thought Adrianna glancing at her watch. l should have shopped earlier as planned after going to the bookshop, but then best laid plans go awry, mostly due to Perry and Buddy's unexpected antics.

Still, I am not late, thought Adrianna, hoping she would get parking close to the food store before collecting Emily. Afterwards, she drove by the pier at the coast and onwards towards the marina.

The sparkling sun blinding her vision and at the same time reflecting the stunning vista across the horizon at sunset as the clouds dispersed after the earlier rain shower. She could see the majestic mountain and its craggy terrain towering above the glistening ocean and islands beyond.

A view that instantly reminded Adrianna of the writing trip to the islands yet to be organised. But there was lots of time as summer was a couple of months away. A perfect break, thought Adrianna, as the islands are the most unspoiled and spiritually uplifting places in the world.

She remembered earlier trips to the islands, and was always surprised by the diverse birds, animal and plant species that populated exposed and sheltered areas. The grey seals and their young played on the craggy rocks and rolled in the bladderwrack, sea moss and thong weed. Various flocks of migratory birds like fulmars, peregrine falcon, snow owls, skuas, herring gulls and barnacle geese, all swarmed the rocky, sandy, sheltered and exposed coastline of the islands, to feed on an abundance of kelp, sea grass and bladderwrack.

And on a sunny day, the mind and senses were instantly calmed by the perfume scent of native flora and fauna like the wild thyme, fairy flax, pyramid orchids, daisies, eyebright, sea pansies and low coralline thistle that dotted every available space on the horizon and provided a rich colourful tapestry, all created by nature.

It's not surprising folks were drawn to such tranquil outposts – in fact everyone from the botanist and birdwatcher to the stressed out business executive, the fun fashionistas on photo shoots to those lost and looking for direction or down time, found a reason to return. The sporty active and fun loving folk enjoyed the surf, sailing and festival party time on the islands and the creative type found inspiration for their next book, picture or design project.

In fact Giles is certain that after spending a summer on one of the Islands after hectic LA he found fresh inspiration for his all seasons Nautical and Floral collection that was a sell-out global success, and the traditional knitwear and junior collection was popular all year round. We joked that my book was really the inspiration behind the sell-out collection, after I suggested young and old just need dress for the environment. And after all, the ocean, mountains, meadows and woodlands are all part of our natural environment. So wearing appropriate seasonal clothing in these natural environments and you're comfortably covered. "Absolutely, I agree," said Jake smiling, and I forgot ...until the invitation arrived and I sent best wishes.

Then almost by chance, I saw the reviews that exploded onto social media about a sell-out collection, praising the natural fabric mix of wool, linen, cotton and tweed. The reversible design detail of the outerwear, the tailoring of the suits and versatility of the separates. That all worked seamlessly from a meeting in the boardroom to brunch at the coast, or a weekend picnic in the meadow or woodlands...and I just knew, without seeing, saying or doing anything else...this was the collection inspired by life on the islands, nature and the natural environment of our connected island nation.

Bathed by the wild Atlantic Ocean spray in summer and lashed too by the thundering waves of stormy winter seas, steeped in ancient customs and craftsmanship. The island communities are a last bastion in many parts of our national heritage, not least our language, making our visit social, cultural and entertaining. We could take the large boat from the pier close by or the traditional small Currach, which was used by native islanders and their fishermen folk in years gone by.

Oh there's Emily, just closing her door, Adrianna waved as she pulled over and stopped the car; both girls greeted each other. "Perfect timing," said Adrianna – "have you heard from the others." "Beth just texted me to say she and Deborah would be there by seven pm," said Emily. "Great," said Adrianna as she turned the car to make their way back.

9

CITY LIFE AWAY

Adrianna works and studies for part the year in the city. This time she is going to visit and stay with her cousin Rebecca and will take Buddy along. Rebecca also has a puppy called Bret that she shares with her boyfriend Fabio. At the weekend, Adrianna and Rebecca will go to visit her uncle in the country. Uncle Ben also has a big farm, stables and a paddock too. Over the stone-wall with windows to the side of the farm, is the palace, almost hidden in the trees and surrounded by beautiful woodland grasses, flora and fauna, where her Royal Highness lives with the Prince and Princesses.

Adrianna works in a very large office building, the front part is shaped like a large dome and the back part of the building towers into the sky. Her office is on the second floor in the dome towards the front of the building. The office has very large windows overlooking a giant water fountain.

Buddy is sometimes scared in this new environment as everything is so very different. Each day, Rebecca or Adrianna take Brett and Buddy for a walk.

On one occasion, Rebecca stopped by on her day off with Buddy and Brett to meet Adrianna for lunch and they waited by the huge water fountain. While Rebecca was checking her phone, Brett lay down by the fountain, but the curious Buddy was observing everything around him in awe.

There were so many different people of every colour, shape and size coming and going. Most if not all were very smart in business suits with bags. Some folks passed by carrying files, others laughing and talking, more serious folks rushing by speaking on their phones or checking their watches, while getting into cars and speeding quickly away.

Buddy saw the postman, but he had a lot more letters and a much bigger bag than the one that delivered the mail back home.

Suddenly, Adrianna appeared, also checking her watch. Buddy danced around impatiently. "Hi everyone," said Adrianna as she patted Buddy, "I am exactly on time and time is money," said Adrianna. Rebecca laughed. "You are right and money makes the world go around, especially in these parts as there are so many banks everywhere."

The girls had lunch at the outdoor café overlooking the river by the promenade Excitedly, Rebecca started telling Adrianna about the email she got from Katie and Jamie inviting her to come and stay at their Chateau and Vineyard in France.

The invitation is such perfect timing as it would fit in well with my plan for a two week language and cultural programme in France and you are invited also," said Rebecca. "That's wonderful, as I could do with a break to improve my language skills too," said Adrianna.

"There is lots of time to plan," said Rebecca. "Mentioning plans, I have to let the folks know what time we will be arriving at the weekend. Fabio will be coming on the Saturday I think, but will be with a shooting party and won't be around very much," said Rebecca.

"That's fine," agreed Adrianna, "if I get delayed with work, I can take the train and you can drive with Buddy and Brett." Adrianna suddenly checked her watch "Oh my god – the time," she exclaimed! "I have to dash back as my team have an important meeting and client presentation this afternoon." Both girls said goodbye and at the same time Rebecca's mobile phone rang, as Adrianna made her way up the steps to her office on the second floor.

She could tell it was Fabio, as Rebecca was fully focused and attentive as always, every time she hears or sees him. Thankfully, I am not on level thirty she thought to herself - I will take the stairs as it will be quicker, and I can get back to my desk to ensure everything is organised for the meeting.

Adrianna passed quickly through the gate that was open admitting a deliveryman and hurried across the main foyer, which is a busy thoroughfare through to the wide stairwell at the side. As she ascended the stairs, she heard loud voices shouting, "stop that puppy, stop that puppy", "how did he get in here". Adrianna stopped instantly and turned around alarmed - she then saw Buddy racing up the stairs towards her panting.

"Buddy what are you doing? You should not be here," said Adrianna, the security man then approached her saying "Miss – puppies, dogs or any type of animal are not allowed into our offices – can I see your security pass, as you should be using the main elevator entrance"?

"Sir I am very sorry, I decided to take a short cut as I needed to get to my desk quickly," exclaimed Adrianna, "I had no idea access was restricted and it will not happen again." "I left Buddy with my cousin Rebecca after lunch and he must have slipped away somehow and followed me here.

I will take Buddy back outside, but may I please stop by my desk to quickly check email to ensure the I have relevant papers and research material for the client presentation? I will also call Rebecca so she will be waiting by the front entrance to take Buddy."

"Ok, Ok but this is the only time I can let you use the side entrance and it goes without saying puppies are not allowed inside the building." "Believe me Sir, I was more shocked than you, Buddy managed to do this. It will never happen again," said Adrianna.

When Adrianna approached her desk with Buddy, she could see her boss Edwin in the large glass-fronted meeting room with some of the team.

As soon as he saw her approaching, he came out, the others all looking out at the same time. "Ah there you are Adrianna," said Edwin who then stopped suddenly, pointing at Buddy and glaring back at Adrianna, "the puppy, where, I mean why he is here?"

"Actually not now – I have the papers, and research data. The visuals are fine, but I need three extra copies and your own set, as Milly is out right now and we have ten minutes. I hope you are up to speed and clear on the key points," said Edwin. "Sure," but first I have to take Buddy out of the building, he followed me back after lunch," explained Adrianna. Milly then appeared and started to pat Buddy and make a big fuss. Edwin cut right in with "oh there you are Milly, can you help Adrianna as we have less than 10 minutes before our clients arrive?"

Edwin had returned from an earlier Board meeting with his usual demanding tone, except everything on his radar had a new level of urgency. Looking for this report, that project update, material for forthcoming conferences, the road show and the list went on.

This time it was the climate reports. "I need everyone's report by Friday morning, as this information is now critical to how much money we will invest in any region globally," said Edwin. "Correct," said Ulrich van Hagan, Edwin's boss who just stopped by as he was leaving for the airport to give Edwin the client feedback report.

"Do you know Edwin, unpredictable and extreme weather conditions have cost our business and the businesses we invest in billions over the last five years"? Even though some experts are not convinced, possibly because they don't believe the scientists, or they live in regions that have not experienced adverse and unusual climatic conditions.

We know that unpredictable and extreme weather conditions have affected crops and harvesting yields, driving up costs and reducing profits margins for many businesses," quipped Ulrich.

"Last year it was beer producers complaining about the shortage of hops due to the poor harvest because of extreme weather conditions, this year growers fret about a vegetable shortage, other times the viniculture industry is concerned about grape quality, after a poor harvest. Further south the olive, fig, saffron and other crop yields of fruit and nuts are lower than expected. As a result, you and I pay more for such fresh produce when we eat in the restaurant or shop at the supermarket.

We are hearing more in recent times about the shortages of other produce like wheat, soya, sugar and cocoa being impacted, so climate change is a local and global issue for our business," said Ulrich.

"The flooding on our own doorstep from non-stop winter downpours that prevented folks from getting to work or having to take time off to clear up the mess, is an immediate example not to mention the cost.
And we've are seeing similar events in areas of United States in the last couple of years also, where extreme weather conditions have caused untold damage and destruction to communities.

There are also more frequent wildfires around the globe, due to the rise in temperatures, especially in dry, hot climates. Warmer temperatures are causing the earlier melting of snow, which also affects glacier movement, leaving less water in the soil when the weather gets warmer into the summer season. This has happened already in my native country in regions close to where I grew up.

Across Africa and India, a late monsoon season and extended periods of drought can wipe out certain crops, creating a shortage of food and higher priced commodities.

Global Warming is causing rising sea levels and forcing communities to relocate, especially those folks living in low lying coastal areas. Warming waters and pollution, also affects marine biodiversity and is altering livelihoods too, as fishermen can no longer fish in local waters.

Global climate change has caused more damage in economic and financial terms in many regions than natural disasters like earthquakes, volcanic eruptions or tsunami's. So we need to seriously consider the insurance cost impact of climate change across all regions, especially those we have invested in," said Ulrich.

"We have to invest more in green technology and less in fossil fuels which are the main culprits of global warming as they create high pollution and smog levels, especially in large cities and industrial zones.

I had to wear a mask just to breathe on an earlier trip to Asia, with some companies having to close for one, maybe two days a week, cars were banned for a couple of days in the week to reduce pollution levels, schools were also closed too for a time and folks advised to stay indoors.

Many suffered ill health and respiratory difficulties because of such high levels of pollution or harmful particles in the air. Resulting in increased health and business costs, and a contributing factor to global warming so we need to rapidly take action," said Ulrich.

"The reports should be on your desk by Friday," said Edwin – "great," replied Ulrich. Just then he was interrupted by his phone, on answering said"thank you, I'm on my way".
"I will review the reports when I get back, so see you then Edwin."
"Have a good trip Ulrich."

Edwin, then clutching the report and scanning it nervously, started to speak in his usual urgent tone as he hovered close to Julie's desk. "Where is everyone?
Don't my team realise their pay cheque depends getting everything right for our clients, and this starts with being on time. God what do they teach them in business school these days?"
You learn the importance of good time-keeping in school for god's sake, never mind college. My daughter is ten years old, and even she knows the importance of good time-keeping. Her wall planner actually confuses me, with detailed timings for school and extra-curricular activities," said Edwin.

"Julie, do me a favour," snapped Edwin – "can you try to reach our team members in Asia, Brazil, North America, United Arab Emirates, Africa and Europe to ensure they are on the line for the conference call. Use my office and we will continue from the conference room," said Edwin.
"Ok," said Julie, dropping her papers on her desk, exasperated as she

made her way in despair to Edwin's office. "When all are on the line, can you remind them of the climate reports and send an email to the Infrastructure Development team," said Edwin.

"I know my team are working in different time zones, and its midnight in Tokyo, late evening or early morning the other locations, but they all agreed to be available and this is a global business," said Edwin impatiently. "And where is Adrianna," asked Edwin, again checking and silencing his iPhone, at the same time reaching for his papers on the oak sideboard to the right of his desk.

Milly was just stepping away from her desk as Edwin went by the conference room. "Ah Milly," said Edwin "can you try and find Adrianna, I need her here as she is presenting and there will be questions. And can you please be on standby just in case we need additional support or there are technical issues?"

"I have already asked IT to have a member of the team available." Well remind them again" said Edwin, "as I don't want any further blips or embarrassments today." "Sure - I will let them know," said Milly.

Buddy thought this was the strangest place in the world, buzzing with activity.

One entire wall looked like giant movie screen with constantly changing pictures, drawings, numbers and text. And what an unfriendly, demanding man! Buddy decided.

There were people in what looked like rooms with windows from floor to ceiling, others sitting looking at coloured screens, some talking on the telephone in strange voices he didn't understand even when they laughed and other more serious folk striding past with files towards the main doors by the elevators.

As he made his way across the office with Adrianna, he could see a couple of people standing getting drinks and, talking seriously while others were laughing close to where Milly was making copies.

To the right of the coffee making area was another longer screen, but this time only showing large red and blue text. As Buddy came closer to the screen, he could hear music and a voice that read each point aloud, going silent again, as the same text continued to appear.

OUR BUSINESS PRIORITIES:

OUR PEOPLE, CUSTOMERS and COMMUNITY
CYBER SECURITY
LEGAL and BUSINESS REGUALTIONS
HEALTH and SAFETY
CLIMATE CHANGE (REDUCING OUR GLOBAL FOOT PRINT)

Adrianna stopped for a moment to help Milly out before going to the main the main entrance with Buddy.
She then called her cousin Rebecca, asking her to be at the main exit to take Buddy. Rebecca was so glad Adrianna had Buddy; as she was frantically trying to reach her, but could not get through. Adrianna

could not always get a signal on her mobile in certain parts of the building.

Buddy rushed through with Adrianna, knowing well at this point he had been a naughty boy and was in the wrong place. I should have stayed with Rebecca and Brett, he thought.

Adrianna now seemed so stressed and in such a hurry, he could tell by how tight she held his lead and her long-hurried strides, but then everyone seemed in a hurry, rushing by with bags, or glancing through documents, checking their phones or watches.

"Buddy I have no time for this nonsense, you are such a naughty boy," said Adrianna, pausing momentarily as she went by the cafeteria to get some water but decided against. She could see two chefs in their pristine whites pointing out from an equally pristine food counter, as she made her way with Buddy into the foyer to the security gates. Adrianna then asked the security guard to open the gate so Buddy could exit. The security guard stood looking at Buddy in amazement and then at Adrianna perplexed, she could tell. "I am sorry Sir, but he followed me in by accident," said Adrianna. "You can exit here Miss," said the security guard.

Adrianna's mobile was ringing at the same time as she hurried through the gate with Buddy. On answering nervously, a panicked voice saying, "where are you"? It was Milly on the line. "I'm on my way," she exclaimed.

Everyone is so stressed out right now, and I am not where I need to be, in fact, right now, am not even in the zone and LATE for a key client presentation thought Adrianna - which is not good from any viewpoint. And where is Rebecca? Instantly relieved she could see Rebecca and Brett though the glass-fronted foyer standing just to the side of the revolving doors. "Adrianna, I'm so sorry, he managed to slip away. "Its fine, don't let him escape again – I have to get back quickly as this is such an important project and the clients have arrived already," said Adrianna. "Sure thing, good luck and see you later," replied a Rebecca.

Adrianna knew she was right – as this was a major global cultural and educational project involving government and private sector investment. It would be such a win if our team get selected to develop and manage the project.

Buddy watched Adrianna race back to catch the open elevator to her office. When she returned to her desk, she could see the clients were already assembled in the round office. "Oh there you are," said Milly, "you had better go in - or do you need to freshen up? "Probably, but I had better go and join the meeting immediately as I am already late." Taking her papers quickly, Adrianna glanced through the agenda and the revised timings - thinking she really did need time to de-stress and regain her composure before her turn came to speak.

At the same time, Buddy was making his way back along the river through the park with Brett and Rebecca. She was also in a hurry like everyone in the city, as she rushed to collect Doug and Cassie from school.

Buddy was sometimes nervous in the city, as everything was so very different and there was so much going on with lots of people everywhere and all ignoring Buddy who wanted to stop and be friends, stare or follow.

And there were so many times Buddy just stopped and stared at the constant speeding flow of cars, the tall busses filled with rows of people looking out, or the loud, fast, and sometimes slow-moving trains with bells ringing as they went by.

Buddy couldn't wait for Adrianna to release his lead so he could race around in the park sniffing the grass as he always did back home in the meadow and woodlands.

But walking or running in the park was very different to the meadow thought Buddy. For one thing, the grass in the park was much shorter than the meadow. There were lots of boys and girls walking through or playing ball, others sitting by the trees laughing and talking. Some riding their bikes or walking their dogs and some smiled as if wanting to be friends.

One time Adrianna stopped at the cafe by the lake for a coffee. From here, Buddy had a good view of the lake and everyone quickly passing by. He saw boys and girls on skates, some jogging and others walking with small children in buggies.

Suddenly Buddy started barking loudly, startling Adrianna who was making her way from the food counter with coffee and cookies.

Adrianna then saw familiar faces in the distance – it was Rebecca, Fabio and Brett.

The friends exchanged greetings and gathered around the table, laughing and talking about their day including Buddy's escape to Adrianna's world of work and high powered deal making along with weekend plans for their visit to Uncle Ben's in the country, before heading off again. Rebecca and Fabio were going shopping and Adrianna was going home to catch up on some study for her project.

Buddy was always sad when the weather was cold and rainy, as Adrianna or Rebecca would not take Brett or himself for a walk. Brett often played with Rebecca's knitting wool that sometimes made its way to the living room floor;

Buddy would just sit in the conservatory peering out at the large raindrops splashing against the window before going to sleep, so long as nothing new, strange or different caught his eye, like the jet planes circling as they made their dissent to the airport. Or the louder more urgent, fast moving search and rescue or emergency helicopter as it transited like a flickering star into the night sky beyond, oftentimes startling Buddy as he dozed off to sleep.

10

THE WEEKEND

At Uncle Ben's and Aunt Rose's, Buddy always looks forward to the weekend, but sometimes misses Perry and Bow back home in the village. Uncle Ben's farmyard is big and he has stables a paddock and a huge barn too. Adrianna and Rebecca go riding in the paddock with their cousin Cory and Camilla. Camilla makes a big fuss of Buddy and he barks when she gallops around the paddock.

Aunt Rosie always baked delicious cookies and biscuits for tea and even Buddy and Brett get to taste some. Adrianna said Aunt Rose was the best baker in the world as her chocolate chip cookies, brownies and ginger bread tasted so good.

Uncle Ben and Aunt Rose go to the Summer Fete each year on the village green. There are always lots of beautiful crafts, delicious homemade foods, and a huge merry-go-round, which the children love.

At Christmas, the castle is magical. There is a giant Christmas tree on the front lawn with a huge star at the top.

The week before Christmas there is carol singing by the huge tree and Santa's grotto is all-aglow with little boys and girls hurrying excitedly through the castle gates with their letters for Santa.

On Christmas morning, Aunt Rose and Uncle Ben and the family always go to church before going home for Christmas lunch with their guests. Other folks go to the synagogue, mosque, temple or shrine to pray and worship on their holy days of celebration and remembrance.

Aunt Rose wanted the girls to go to the outdoor art exhibition by the river on Sunday, before going back to the city. She knew Adrianna and Rebecca loved art and they could also take Brett and Buddy along unlike most if not all art galleries.

Buddy liked Aunt Rose and Uncle Ben's house, it was so much more spacious than the little apartment in the City and there were so many rooms, he especially liked the huge entrance hall where Aunt Rose always greeted them, further along, to the side of the stairs, stood a tall bookcase.

Buddy could tell Adrianna was impressed by the selection of books in the large book case. There were books with covers showing serious, sad and happy people. And on the top shelf there were rows of dark coloured books that all looked the same

The next shelf had books on bees, butterflies and birds. And further along more colourful books on roses, plants and posies.

On the middle shelf there were books about fabrics and wool on how to do, make and create various garments and accessories. Others larger books had covers with delicious cookies, breads and biscuits, jellies and cakes. She saw a storybook like the one Rebecca read to Cassie and

Dougie one time after school about the boy who went on an adventure to discover everything from the start to the end of the rainbow. And a silver shiny book called CODE to re-shape the world, that reminded Adrianna of a story she read about a little girl who got lost in the forest and found a magic coding school where the students were busy designing and creating code to literally change our planet.

"The main objective of our CODING class is obviously to learn to code and then to improve, enhance and make more efficient systems," explained the Tutor Zachie in the story. Eliminate the baddies like pollution and poisons from our planet and speed up how everything works, so the universe becomes instant. In fact, CODE creates a parallel, instant world of systems that work in harmony to operate our universe. Zachie likened the concept to the transition or development of a coffee bean to instant coffee. And eventually, they would create communities of robots, who look, act and communicate just like humans, only much more skilled and powerful in every way," explained Zachie, in that CODING story.

"CODING is key to improving our world explained," Zachie to his students. Emphasising their key focus was enhancing the external environment, to create healthy lives, and healthy, efficient processes and systems. The CODING project phase II will focus on healthy lives, to ensure everyone achieved life-long health and health care through efficient, accurate test systems that enable speedy resolution for infants, young and old alike," said Zachie. The story made for an interesting read and definitely inspired Adrianna to take a CODING class which impressed everyone, especially the new App she designed as part of the course CODING project. This surprised Rebecca, as technology never interested her cousin, but they all agreed that coding was changing the world. Camilla said everyone is coding or wants to code, because this is the new way to create, design, and to rework existing systems.

"Wow, well done said Fabio. "Thank you," said Adrianna. The app is called 'Free to Focus' and will connects everyone to their particular free time or leisure activity, holistic health and professional career areas.

"When is it available," asked Rebecca. It should be live next week I hope, unless my tutor finds errors and I need to revise something," said Adrianna. "How exciting, I cannot wait to try it out," said Fabio. "It's just regular stuff, as there are millions of apps out there, you know that," said Adrianna.

"It's like Camilla said earlier, the entire universe is now reliant on technology code in one form or another, to manage systems and processes, think, analyze, formulate and execute a range of activities and transactions, even though junior camp was just about finding fun ways to work and create with code," said Adrianna. "True," said Fabio "but we are still impressed by your project." It's so very exciting," exclaimed Rebecca. "You will let us know when it's definitely available online," asked Camilla. "Absolutely," replied Adrianna.

Buddy hated returning on Sunday to the small apartment and bright lights of the crowded, busy city. How his life had changed - there were so many things to see and places to explore which were new and different in the city from his quieter life back home with his friendly and unfriendly neighbours.

11

FABIO'S AND THE MOVIES

Fabio invited Adrianna and Rebecca around one Sunday afternoon for a 3D movie experience. Brett and Buddy went along too as it was within walking distance. Nothing could prepare Buddy for their visit to Fabio's high-tech hub, which he called home. It was in effect, a large wooden floored warehouse apartment, with bare walls and what looked like tree trunks for seating in spaces by the walls.

It was bigger than Rebecca's apartment in every sense with a long table and breakfast bar in the kitchen space. Huge stairs leading to a gallery area where Fabio's bedroom, bathroom and storage area was located. The entire roof appeared to be covered in glass. The strangest room of all was Fabio's studio, which was to the right as you went through the front door.

When he switched on the lights they sparkled from the floor in ever changing colours – Buddy had never seen lights in the floor before. "Fabio likes to show off," whispered Rebecca to Adrianna as he was activating a large screen and juggling the various system controls. "That is such a fantastic screen," said Adrianna,

"Isn't it - look I can enlarge the view, bring the images closer, check my email, my social media pages, get a full weather up-date and order a pizza," explained Fabio, as he continued flicking to the next fancy feature before switching on the main TV/Video screen, while still juggling various controls at the same time.

"That looks so impressive, but complicated," said Adrianna. "Oh really it's simple, I am just trying to enhance the visual effects, so you can get the best view," replied Fabio.

The overhead light continued to change colours and at times darkened out completely, emerging like stars in the roof.

Buddy was almost hypnotized just looking at those lights continually change colour as he made himself comfortable under Adrianna's seat. Brett was positioned on the rug in front of the large screen his head resting on his paws, starting to look either sleepy or bored, despite the interaction of lights and the high-tech overview Fabio was working hard to create for everyone.

"I am assisting with the production of a new movie called 'The Giant's Precious Stone' and here is the initial trailer and a short summary," said Fabio.

"Brilliant," said Adrianna. "It's very exciting," said Rebecca. "The movie storyline tells of a giant who had a precious stone that he kept hidden away in a vault at the top of his castle. The precious stone had magic and medicinal powers that could ward off diseases, evil spirits and punish unjust acts," explained Fabio.

'One day when the giant was out hunting with his friends a large eagle noticed the stone glistening in the sun and went to investigate.

The eagle slipped in through the small window of the vault at the top of the castle and snatched the precious stone with his long beak, and flew away across the lake, meadow, hills and valleys, to his nest high up in the trees at the top of the mountain.

Soon the giant noticed the precious stone was missing and he got very angry, summoning all his subjects, useful friends, and neighbours, to find out if they knew anything of the missing stone. All swore allegiance, pleaded their innocence and convinced the giant they knew nothing about the theft of his precious stone.

"We will have to send out a search party and visit all the villages, towns and cities along the way. I know my precious stone glistens in the sunlight, and it has the powers to punish evil, so who knows, it may save itself. If any unjust or evil acts are carried out, my precious stone has the power to ward off and protect from evil deeds, it also has the power to cure sickness and disease. So even though we will start to search, I will also be patient too," said the distraught giant, "as my precious stone has supernatural powers. So when I hear of heroic deeds to punish evil and cure disease and sickness, I will know instantly this is the powers of my precious stone at work".

Fabio continued to explain the story. "In the mean time, the eagle took the precious stone to his nest and placed it with the little eagle chicks that were just hatched.

The mother eagle appeared with food in her beak, while the precious stone sparkled in the evening sun, distracting the chicks from their food".

"There is more obviously, but I cannot tell you how the movie develops or the outcome, because I am sworn to secrecy. And as it is, you have seen and know too much," said Fabio. "Oh sure thing your secret is safe with me, besides I will be heading back home in a couple of weeks. Maybe we'll be able to see the finished movie at the cinema," said Adrianna.

"I hope so, but the company I work for is just a small production company, I am not sure what their marketing schedule or production plans are, but I will let you know," said Fabio. "Great," said Adrianna. "I already know someone who will be famous. "Hardly, as this is just a small project," replied Fabio.

"Well producing a movie has got to create some fame. Producers are usually pretty powerful people in the movie business you know," said Adrianna.

"Rebecca, just think about it – you could be mingling with the stars after walking down the red carpet in Hollywood glamour and glitz style," laughed Adrianna.

"What a dream even fairy-tale?" sighed Rebecca, "can you imagine, super efficient nanny to glamour girl for a day." "Excuse me," said Fabio to Rebecca, "I think that would make you glamour girlfriend." "That's true, I might even get offered a part in your movie and finally use my training to eventually live the dream, now that would, be an even better outcome," smiled Rebecca.

And then I will know two famous people, a movie star and director, so my script may just make it on to the big screen," suggest Adrianna smiling. "A hint of ambition, brains and talent...I like it," replied Fabio. Let's enjoy today and celebrate our dreams for tomorrow," suggested Fabio as all settled in for the actual movie moment.

By this time, Buddy was totally enthralled as he had never seen such a big TV before and the overhead coloured lights made his world new and very different again, until suddenly there were no lights, only the very large movie screen that totally amazed Buddy.

Brett was almost asleep, but perked up once he smelled the delicious chocolate chip cookies and other savoury and sweet treat Fabio was passing around, that everyone tucked into, as they got comfortable for the 3-D movie experience.

The screen now looked bigger and closer and everyone was wearing weird glasses. How very strange, thought Buddy. Then he suddenly heard a yelping sound and cast his eyes back to the big screen again.

Two white puppies emerged running through a garden, instantly reminded him of Perry the poodle and Otes racing in the meadow back home, as they were both the same colour.

Buddy started to then wonder if Perry ever missed him, and if he was getting on well with Bow. He didn't have time to miss them since arriving in the city, as his life has been very different. With so many strange sights coming and going and these alone occupied his day.

Then the actual movie moment at Fabio's finally arrived. A movie called 'Planet Real or Imagined', about a couple of techie friends who won a prize for their project idea to design SMART sports shirts for the college basketball team to improve their overall performance and win more games in the league.

The SMART shirt design had reached the testing stage and results were positive for the garment that was equipped with health, fitness, performance monitoring and a range of connective features.

Jorge was a key member of the key technology designers who mysteriously went missing at a crucial time in the project, which confused everyone including Jorge himself.

Jorge was in a deep slumber and felt aliens took him to a distant planet way out there in the galaxy. He imagined being woken up with an urgent message flashing on his smart watch saying, "we picked up your signal on our planet, please identify yourself."

He tried to stop the alarm, but the SMART watch turned red and then blue. Still unable to stop the loud alert alarm, he removed the watch, and left it on the sideboard. Suddenly the watch was smoking and then disintegrated into dust.

Jorge woke up early and went into his father's office to use his computer to search for information about the possibility of life other planets in the universe. He knew that nothing unusual was found so far to suggest there was life on another planet. His father's files were password protected and classified, and he could not find his SMART watch.

Knowing this was serious and mysterious; he decided for now to keep it a secret from his family, even though his father was a scientist and on a team that investigated areas of the galaxy for signs of extra-terrestrial life.

Then one evening after testing, end of semester exams as he make his way back home from band practise, suddenly a huge star shaped spaceship set down in the park in front of the ice-cream parlour blocking his path.

Sliding doors opened and an alien who introduced himself as Lufphy stepped out of the star shaped spaceship, invited Jorge aboard. The second alien called Prajkery said they picked up a signal and traced it to his window by the tall willow trees. So Jorge assumed they probably knew he was holding the entire project programme coding and design test results in his garage, which had become the co-ordination centre for the project.

Jorge was intrigued and awe struck at the sight of the blue circular interiors of the spaceship and endless control panels, with a multitude of dials and switches that went full circle, and was manned by two robots. He was seated comfortably opposite the two aliens, one continuously checked his wrist devices and the other was reading charts and checking the control panel from time to time. He decided they looked almost like regular people apart from their ears that protruded and their pointed chin, which gave them elfin features.

As the spaceship transited though the galaxy into the unknown world, I could see a million stars lighting up the dark universe. I remember seeing the red planet and a very large planet partly obscured by fog, then a star shaped planet that almost blinded our vision lighting up the entire spaceship. We then seemed to gain altitude after passing the blue planet, and dipped again before arriving at what I thought was our final destination.

"We are please you accepted our invitation as you are a very talented young man to create such a powerful code," said Prajkery. "That is part of my project to launch a SMART shirt for our school team," replied Jorge. "We are very interested in finding out more details Jorge about your plans and planet earth," said Prajkery.

"My project details are top secret," uttered Jorge. "Jorge, we are not just interested in your project plans, we want to find out about the world you live in and the folk who inhabit this Earth world.
As our sources tell us you humans on earth plan to visit our planet in the not too distant future, so we want to ensure we are prepared for such visits to our land.
After all, new moons and planets in the galaxy and cosmos, are constantly being discovered by you Earth people. And your scientists

are inching ever closer to discovering all there is to know about new planets and their moons, from the various global space projects," said the deep throated alien called Lufphy.

"These developments have alarmed the higher Gods and made them nervous as they believe it's just a matter of time before our planet is discovered. Of course, artificial intelligence has made communication easier and especially so for tracking and connecting with outside forces and to view specific targets of interest, particularly those with ambitions to visit our planet or find our people.
Like the various agencies and of course your father's work, the people he works for and other nation states on a similar path, to find life beyond planet earth, or make new discoveries.

And although we have no evidence to suggest our people will be harmed, or indeed that such missions will ever prove successful, there is always the fear such determined efforts will succeed.

Our Gods and the higher panel are disturbed by such possibilities and are insisting we take every measure possible to secure our planetary parameters," said Prajkery.

"Celest, Daughter of the higher God is at a crucial time in her studies, and needs additional information for her research project, so information directly from an Earth person will ensure she impresses her father and achieve the required high marks for detail and initiative," said Lufphy.

When we got off the star shaped spaceship, we then boarded a long tunnel type vehicle that glided along and then gained height, whisking us through a midnight blue silver sky to a sparkling city on a hill. On arrival at the final destination, and before leaving the spaceship, Jorge was given a shield to wear under his jacket, and was told it would neutralise foreign particles and gases that were incompatible with the human body systems. The mask was optional but necessary if I experienced breathing difficulties.

Jorge could not believe his eyes, this new planet was colder, but everything was vast, automatic, instant and a regular a to b SMART thoroughfare.
There was clothing that propelled you into the air and enabled you to land at the touch of a control button on the sleeve. Other clothing styles made you slim and colour co-ordinated, lit up in the dark, gave directions and played music. The beachwear enabled you to float, swim or sunbath and then converted to a dress or trousers.

"You now can also see firsthand how our planet operates Jorge, in fact there are so many examples of the project you are working on now to create SMART clothing. All our clothing is ten times more advanced and is regular wear for old and young alike. You may even get some new inspiration for your project," said Prajkery.

"Our project is now at the testing stage and almost complete," said Jorge. "We have all the resources required and have collaborated with local technology companies for advice and input at each phase of the project. I am still not sure why you are interested in my project, as you appear to have a much more advanced SMART selection of everything," said Jorge.

"You are of interest like a couple of others on our internal radar because you are from Earth obviously, are bright and smart enough to have created a code we can read and it works as we were able to locate you with precision and also similar to codes used in our 'functional clothing'.

"Some of your people are also trying to locate our planet, but so far have been unsuccessful.
After all, your father and his friends have spent a lot of time and effort trying to discover life on other planets, no doubt in preparation for such future voyages.
In fact our sources tell us, some folk have already signed up to make the journey into the unknown on our planet," said Lufphy.

"My father's work is classified and I never get to see what he does and I am not interested in what he does, so I cannot help you," pleaded a panicked Jorge.

"You must also realise, you have the wrong guy and you've made a mistake, as my other friends are really talented and super intelligent guys," said Jorge.
"If fact, it was Kyle," said Jorge hesitantly, unsure if he should name names or divulge any information at this point. "How do you mean," asked Lufphy, as he looked around at the other two.

"My other friend on the project called Kyle wrote the code," said Jorge. "But you are part of the project, as the signal went directly through to your window in the garden," said Lufphy. "That's my garage," said Jorge.

"Either way – you are our person," said the alien called Prajkery. "You are a native, gone or going to college and can explain or demonstrate what we are likely to expect from folk who decide to visit our planet from Earth in the next maybe 5, but certainly 10 to 15 years from now. "I have no idea who's planning to visit your planet now or in the future," said Jorge, "so you've made a mistake."

"I assure you Jorge, we have made no mistake, we have done our research, know who you are and what we want to achieve and find out about you Earth people," said Prajkery.

"My interests are definitely around my current project," said Jorge nervously. "I must get back to Earth as my friends and family will miss me and start to panic. I also have end of semester exams and our SMART shirt launch to prepare for in early spring," said Jorge. "Do not worry, Jorgk" ..."its Jorge."

"Jorge we will have you back safe and well after a short fact-finding task for Celest, the higher God's daughter, and a brief interview, which is really a compare and contrast task, to ensure our files have the correct information. Celest secretly harbours the desire to one day live on planet Earth with you humans after an earlier brief visit, and wants material for her project based on a real study of Earth people so she can impress her father, and ensure the correct plans are implemented to protect this planet from discovery into the next millennium.

"We want to avoid hostilities and try first to understand who you earth people are, how you work and operate, live and behave. This way when the time comes for us to meet, we will be better prepared to respond to such voyages of intrusion from Earth," said Prajkery.

"Right now, we are somewhat puzzled by you Earth people wanting to embark on a complete journey into the unknown. And from what we do know, there are no immediate threats or danger, which makes it more difficult to anticipate or prepare for such events.
Your people from Earth are a different substance and have nothing in common with our people or any chance of establishing a meaningful link or lifestyle here. Our higher Gods are already alarmed at news of such plans and are forcing us now to prepare for the worst," explained the alien Prajkery. "Well my friends and I have no interest in your planet or other planets, and we are also a different people, so you've made a mistake," insisted Jorge.

"Jorge, like I said, we have done our research to ensure our plans and predictions prepare us for the future. And even though we are a different people, you may be surprised to learn we have already taken some inspiration from Earth's natural environment to enhance life on our planet. For example, we love the green grass, and have taken and used this in many ways from designing activities for children to smart clothing; it also creates oxygen, which is vital for survival on your planet Earth. The daisies have been copied in a similar way to make smart devices like lighting, and communications systems.

Daisies are also used in food, where we copy their shape for cookies and ice cream. We love the daisy chain idea too as a linking mechanism, which are uses in some of our 'functional' accessories. We have also discovered the health benefits of some plants like your nettle, foxglove, camomile, sunflowers and lavender, for joints, blood, skin, healing and overall health. All are enjoyed on our planet as drink offerings, in candy and skin lotions.

Your autumn and neutral colours are used in clothing for our army, in SMART footwear and in many other internal and external design creations.
Your watches don't just tell the time on our planet, but have been re-designed and enhanced as a key communicational tool, body monitoring system, a signalling system and to lock and unlock various devices, even play music. We have also copied the rainbow for use as lighting along with a colour coded warning system, and the list goes on.

In fact, the Gods were silenced for weeks when we explained how one or two pieces of very powerful tools made from a combination of precious stones, minerals and metals, were all that was required to help keep our planet safe, connected and contented. And of course these systems and programmes are being constantly upgraded and enhanced to deal with unexpected or anticipated threats and to neutralise toxic gases from beyond our planets safe zone," said Prajkery.

"So what do you want from me, as surely you cannot expect me to have the answers or know who intends to visit your planet now or in the future," said Jorge anxiously. "We now want to get a closer look at you Earth people," said Lufphy.

"Here is the simple question manuscript with pictures to assist Celest, daughter of the higher God, with her project work on Planet Earth. All we want you to do is answer the required questions and fill in the gaps and explain the pictures," said Lufphy.

She has already completed projects on the other inner and outer planets and their associated moons orbiting the solar system, and wasn't inspired, especially after seeing activity on planet Earth.

Celest is now at an important point in her studies, and wants to ensure her ideas and information on planet Earth are correct, after earlier fact-finding missions. This is mostly why we met Jorge, and the reason for this recent impulsive voyage to planet Earth," explained Lufphy.

"You see Jorge we experience information not just process and store it during the learning cycle. Our students explore, discover and create new ways of doing things during their studies and where possible, experience a visual overview of the subject matter. They study current events, and neighbouring planetary activity of interest. Students also go back in time visually and forward into the future, suggesting changes and new ways of working and living along the way.
Many are then expected to go forward into the future and create new worlds of existence, to assure the continuity of our superior race

standing in the eyes of the gods," explained Prajkery. "Your input here will ensure we can create and present more accurate information for our junior and senior students, and also assist Celest with her final project work," said Lufphy. So Jorge diligently set about completing the ten page questionnaire with pictures.

"After the task, you also have an excellent opportunity to get some new inspiration, and in a small way explore the world we inhabit. In fact there are stores full of what you call SMART clothing that almost connect to everything in our universe," said Prajkery.

"Can I make my own notes of you apparel, accessories, sportswear and areas of operation?" asked Jorge. "This will not be a problem," said the third blond haired alien, whose name was Starstaz. "You will be accompanied at all times and are free to make whatever notes you choose.

Pictures are not allowed, but it's unlikely your device will work on our planet and we cancelled out our signal path to you earlier and destroyed a device, to protect our identity and existence," said Starstaz. "You mean my SMART watch," suggested Jorge. "Exactly, but you will get a replacement that will function exactly the same," replied Starstaz, who then was summons by a flashing light and intermittent bleep on a similar SMART wrist device. "I must get back...enjoy yourself Jorge," said Starstaz as she immediately left.

The sportswear and performance related gear was awesome. This high performance wear automatically identified your maximum potential, cardio vascular health, muscle strength, stamina levels and instantly produced a fitness rating and training plan. Training and performance results were issued in a similar way and showed on the sleeve area at the press of a button.

Jorge was advised a high level of fitness was required by their army and these performance levels were being increased to coincide with new ground and air defence tactics.

"Our juniors also require the highest performing sportswear to enhance fitness attainment levels, and safeguard from injury or over exertion during training practice and events. We don't just use code in our clothing designs," explained Prajkery, "all our processes are built on science, precision design with engineering and technology to achieve the required outcome for our garments."

The most awesome sight of all was the cars that looked like the inside of a plane cockpit with the amount of controls, screens and buttons. But were all seemingly self-driving regular cars, until they leapfrogged into the air, which I was told was both to avoid obstructions and to reach the next level on their planet.

Then there were huge vehicles with wings that carried a couple of aliens and robots that were flying off. When I asked about them, I was told firmly, this should not be of interest, their people were just on routine and regular daily activity missions.

These appeared to be business projects, as two of the aliens carried files and the other a bag. A robot then emerged to join them with a chart and was flipping the pages as if searching for a particular point or topic, as he walked to the car with wings to join the others, who were now seated behind desks. Jorge was ushered past them quickly through two large Ice cube doors that lead to a snow-white paradise.

First stop was the coffee lounge, but the coffee was white and tasted like vanilla and chocolate with red chocolate beans and a cinnamon topping to finish which was almost perfect thought Jorge, with just the hazelnut syrup missing. There was Ice steak and seeds, granite, chocolate and ice cookies and crystallised carmel jelly sorbet on offer too.

Instead of a menu or food display board, a digital screen of the human anatomy was displayed overhead, with arrows pointing to the relevant suggested food offerings for each part of the body. "As you can see Jorge, our food is functional and nutritional and daily dietary consumption is strictly practised.

If you stand in the request zone, the most suitable food for you personally, flashes on the display board, indicating exactly where and why your body requires the suggested liquid or food combinations for energy, healing, tissue repair, strength building, muscles, digestive-health, cardiac, circulatory or other functions. If your body is out of balance, a red alarm will sound, along with immediate dietary suggestions. Of course, there are the recreational foods like the type you see here in this cafe which are like your ...how do you say...small bites," said Prajkery. "I think you mean snacks," said Jorge. "Exactly Jorge, snacks," said Prajkery smiling.

We then went to see the accessories and shoes, which were also awesome. I was informed they used a combination of old and new materials and particularly liked to combine our wood with their precious metals and stones in the myriad of designs, size, colours and shapes, available on display.

All accessories appeared to have a secondary function and were either fully or part connected. For example some were navigational, others played music, some were equipped with a light and contained complex technology inserts that enabled instant access to IT systems.

Handbags came complete with built in phone, camera, music and video capabilities, a mirror and for security, lit up in the dark.

Some shoe styles were invisible from the ankle and reached the top of the leg, in various styles with fully adjustable heel heights. These were fitted out with all types of sensors, health monitors, navigational and tracking tools.

Our essential mobile communication device provides a selection of instant updates by just pointing the device in the direction you need information. For example, If I stand here, or am entering a new location, when I point my device north, south, east or west, I will automatically receive a selection of 'need to know', 'useful to know' and 'general information' readings about that particular region, along with the usual lists of entertainment venues, restaurants and retail outlets.

My favourite SMART accessories are the 'location lens' that enable you to get an overview of the environment and activity anywhere in the universe with co-ordinates," explained Prajkery. Every kid wants to have one, even though they get to use them for project work in school. Jorge decided they looked like expensive designer sun glasses and were pretty cool.

My next favourite accessory is the 'power pack' that is not just a bag, but can propel you a couple of meters into the air and transport you to your destination. This is particularly useful if in a hurry, the traffic is bad, you are too tired to walk or just don't want to walk," said Prajkery.

And finally the 'body wrap belt' is somewhat like SMART clothing, that is fitted with a combination of health and fitness features, functional features like lights, clock, maps, warning updates and alarms, and then a range of recreational features.

The 'functional' SMART clothing is amazing too, and almost fully connected, where individual pieces are used as diagnostic garments to detect medical conditions, and in a general sense, to provide weather warnings, find directions, enables you to communicate, provide protection, play music, provide coverage and obviously keep you warm. As the 'functional' name suggests Jorge, we use fabric in many ways, but this is not unusual.

As we know from our 'locator lens', fabric has a variety of uses on your planet Earth. Of course for clothing to drape and keep earth folk warm and protected. But there are so many other instances where we have observed how fabric is used.

For example in the home, fabric is used as decorated wall hangings, curtains on the window to ensure privacy, or block out light. In some cultures, fabric prints are used as a warning and to celebrate major life events. In other location, fabric serves as a door and in more remote outposts or in very warm climates, as a house. We know fabric is also used to fly into the sky, in fact we had a near miss on one voyage with such a design and had to move the spaceship to invisible, then rapidly increase altitude, or we would have crashed into the many flying balloons at a location on your planet Earth. And it appears other more formal fabric uses denote status, creative skills and national identity at global events.

So it is fitting our 'functional garments' have also many uses and are fully connected. New fabric designs with enhanced features are being developed all the time, and you may even get some ideas and inspiration for your next SMART design," said Prajkery. "Oh my project is in the final stages, and then I have to focus on my studies, but these clothing designs are awesome," agreed Jorge enthusiastically.

Jorge was shown how they used some earth plants and herbs to create sweet scented lotions and creams. The applicators didn't just dispense or hold one type, but like a multicoloured pen, held about three or four different types of product, one for the face and eyes, the other for the hands and body.

The mirror also acted as an information screen that advised you of the exact shades that worked in accordance with your reflection in the actual mirror, and provided advice on other suitable product offerings.

The packaging technique also saved on storage space and works for everyone," explained Prajkery. "Wow, everything is different," said Jorge.

"Absolutely," said Prajkery in a superior and confident sounding tone, "most of our ideas, systems, procedures and methods are unique and not available or obvious on your planet Earth.

And at party time, everyone selects their celebration colour for the day, which means...actually, here are some pictures on the wall that will give you a better idea. Jorge, was amazed, as the aliens totally covered themselves in colour, some were all gold, others red, some blue ...actually everyone looks amazing in white light," explained Prajkery confidently. "The best part is selection times for party games and the rule is everyone of the same colour, whether groups or pairs come together, which is really fun. As you get to meet and interact with a variety of different people," said Lufphy.

Jorge was now trying hard to appear enthusiastic by such ideas of party games and

colour dressing, suggesting it was similar to a fancy dress party. "Absolutely not," replied Prajkery. "Earth people just show up in unusual costumes and themed dress to mingle at the party, without the grouping or selection element. Like I said, we are a different people with different customs, very strict norms and procedures, but we have fun too," said Prajkery.

"Of course," agreed Jorge, wanting to avoid heated discussions or arguments, as right now the concern was getting back to his own base on planet Earth, in time to complete the college project with his friends.

Suddenly there was a huge alarm, and then emergency beeping at intervals. With instructions to vacate, deactivate, shutdown, keep down and the panic went on.
A huge spotlight was activated that illuminated and magnified every visible particle on their planet. Dozens of Robots and aliens arrived in a long silver tube train at the same time. Some also piled out of cars with wings that were now patrolling higher levels of the planet and obvious in the distance, due to the huge spotlight that moved around.

Starstaz dashed through the ice cube doors followed by two robots to where we were admiring the accessories. "What's wrong," said Prajkery in a nervous voice and with narrowed, darkened eyes... "it's the Gods, the higher panel have detected an unannounced, unidentified intruder and have issued a close down warning across the planet, until such time as the intruder has been identified and captured," said Starstaz.

"I think it may be our Earth study friend, Jorke," said Prajkery..."its Jorge" ..."I know, Jorge you are...I mean we are in trouble," snapped Prajkery. "I thought you cleared such activity with the senior panel," snapped Starstaz. "I keep them informed yes, but on this occasion was uncertain of the outcome, so I decided to get the information and then present our findings from this first-hand encounter with an Earth person. This has been their wish and desire from the start, as they want no mistakes in findings, especially for Celest's final project," said Prajkery.

"Someone must have spied on us," said Prajkery. "Negative - we went off limits and an unusual signal was picked up. Either way, we have a huge problem now and we better find the central control point and alert them as they are in attack mode as we speak. Which means, any unauthorized persons or thing still moving on this level, will die if not instantly identified on their readers," said Starstaz.

"We better go to the emergence vault, which is situated to the left by the main doors.
"Why?" "No questions now," said Starstarz, "luckily I know this place from earlier security drills and we have little time to somehow stop the attack, otherwise we will not escape alive."

"What is that you are wearing on your wrist," asked Starstaz as she moved closer. "It's a precious metals and stone bracelet, the assistant in the other accessory shop gave it to me as a souvenir," replied Jorge.
"That's it - this is what has triggered the alert – they picked up the signal of an intruder or foreign imposter from you wearing this bracelet on our planet, without access clearance. These prepared and polished metals are used in all types of sensors and communication signals on our planet," explained Starstaz.

"I will wear it for now," said Prajkery, "but it will not solve the problem or stop the very imminent attack," snapped Starstaz.

Next thing about 50 robots entered through the ice cube doors and walked passed our location in the vault followed by seemingly one of the gods with about 20 alien folk scanning each area to locate the signal, with their wand shaped device. There was a loud bleeping noise as they went by with the device, that weakened until they returned towards our location, and the bleeping noise started to get louder again. Jorge could feel his heart pounding and thought this was the end for him, there was no escaping.

"We need to get the boy back quickly, but this is an instant and immediate solution to quiet alarms and throw them off this trail," said Starstarz, as she took a slim pointed container from her pocket. This is a temporary measure Jorge, and you will make full recovery," said Starstaz as she sprayed a substance in his face. Jorge was gripped by fear and panic but went limp in an instant. "Great," said Starstaz, "the alarm has stopped."

"How will we account of our sudden departure and swift return? We have no new data or further developments to report from Earth either, apart for some useful information for Celest's study project," said Lufphy.

"Oh for God sake, you can't be serious; you guys are sneaking around for a child. A wide eyed, naive, impressionable teen, almost getting us killed in the process," said a raging Starstarz. "She will impress the Gods, especially her father, and all will be well, trust me," replied Lufphy.

"Right now, I trust you to get us severely punished and almost killed Lufphy – the senior panel will be furious over the unauthorized mission. Along with that, inside sources tell me there is alarm over Celest's interest in Earth and future plans for further research on the actual planet, and for that matter she may have caused the alarm, maybe spied, as she was impressed, if only from a distance by the Earth boy, after seeing him in the cafe that time," said Starstaz.

"We are not allowed to take foreign persons on board the spaceship without authorization and you know this," continued Starstaz. "The only time we break this rule, and go off course is if we encounter Santa, the elves and reindeers, as they sometimes run into difficulty. But this is also risky, as the reindeers are nervous, and find the spaceship alarming, the elves are impatient, and Santa is usually stressed, requiring emergency assistance to reach some far flung destination on planet Earth, before little boys and girls wake up.

Other folks with magic powers also crossed our path, but when we were unwilling to assist their rescue and recovery efforts or co-operate on future projects, they have since disappeared from view.

Even though sources tell us these folks with magic powers reached an inner planet on a single rescue and recovery mission, they are of little concern, as they don't have an army, or location point we can identify or trace on our radar," said Starstaz.

"Enough," said Prajkery, who had just returned from a meeting with the senior panel. "This whole incident makes us look foolish as there were no major useful discoveries, even the data is obsolete and worse still our standing, influence and future prospects in the eyes of the Higher Panel is diminished, as we speak.

They want us to remove all trace of the earth boy, after finding his jacket during the lock-down search. The silver robot warriors were instructed by the higher Gods to return data files from our earlier fact-finding missions to Earth. They threw the files on my desk after the meeting, with a written 'dispose of contents' order in line with our peaceful, super race approach - staring me in the eye as they left the room, and then at each other," said Prajkery.

"So the higher panel not only wants us to remove the contents off our planet and return to source on planet Earth they have also requested we cancel future exploration and research plans. As they are suddenly happy our work is now done and there is nothing to fear for the moment," said Prajkery.

"So not only do we look foolish but we also failed in the eyes of the Gods," said Starstarz.

"Not necessarily, Dialray to the East and Zephes to the North are of more concern now and pose a greater threat. As intelligent sources say they are quickly building defence capabilities and high-tech armies, so this is the other reason planet Earth less of a priority for now," said Lufphy.

"I knew it was a huge mistake, as it forced a change in strategy, regardless of other threats, our acting without authorization was viewed as reckless," said Starstarz.

Suddenly Jorge was awakened by a loud thumping noise, and his phone was ringing at the same time. As he tried to get to the phone it fell onto the floor. The rays of the sun blinding his vision and his two friends peering through the window outside, made Jorge realise he was definitely back on planet earth.

"Hold on," said Jorge, as he struggled out of bed, trying hard to get his brain to work in the here and now. Where have you been, why haven't you been answering your phone," said an anxious Kyle. We need the presentation file," said Hal. "Relax guys, it's Saturday," said Jorge rubbing his eyes at the same time, struggling to grasp their urgency. "It's Monday, and almost 12.30, the project review is at 1pm," said Hal.

"Oh my god, my folks are away and I need to put out the garbage and feed our cat Heebie," said Jorge. "Your cat is having lunch on the lawn," said Kyle. "That's exactly what Mom didn't want," said Jorge, peering out the window at the same time. "At least someone is awake around here," snapped Kyle. "I'm, I mean Heebie is in real trouble, as our neighbour already caught him pouncing on little birds as they fed from their bird table, on other side of our fence, and complained that all the birds had fled, and her grandchildren were disappointed when they came to visit." "I seriously hope she didn't see Heebie this time, because we will both be in big trouble," said Jorge, as he peered out the window again.

"Jorge...Jorge, can't this wait, we need the project file," said Kyle. "Sure, I just need to put this bin outside, actually can you get the door," asked Jorge. "Where have you been," asked Kyle, "nobody has seen you since Thursday." "I was at band practice on Friday," replied Jorge – "well Friday," said Kyle. "Hal has the motifs and the designs ready; but we have to look at the sizing again, as there are new members. The technology company have verified the programme works and is compatible, and even app friendly," said Kyle. Jorge was still trying to register events. "Absolutely guys, I agree," replied Jorge blankly. "Hey, wake up man, how do you mean you agree, where is the schedule and presentation file," asked Hal. "After all, you agreed to email this on Saturday pm so we all had a chance to review and agree on timings," said Kyle in a panicked voice. "Hey, relax guys," said Jorge, "I know where everything is, it's just I was somewhere else ...I think," replied an uncertain Jorge. "That's obvious, but it's Monday Jorge, and we have project deadlines, you know this, in fact you helped set them," said an astonished Kyle.

"I cannot believe you man," said Hal. "You know we all have to pull together and work as a team on this one to meet the target dates." "I think there is no need for coding," said Jorge. "You tell me this now some zillion hours of work later, so what's your alternative," asked Kyle. "Less coding and more science" said Jorge. "That's almost like saying let's re-write the design," said Kyle as his two white puppies sniffed around the room.

At the same, Buddy continued to reminisce on his new and old friends. He liked Brett too, who was now asleep, but wished he was more adventurous and energetic, as at times he reminded him of Bow, who was downright lazy. Especially in the summer when he would mostly sniff around the garden or stretch out and sleep in the sun, never wanting to venture too far. At least Perry the poodle made the effort to join in or tag along, unless he was afraid or too exhausted.

More snacks and drinks were on offer at Fabio's as the movie continued and the team finally reached the top of the college league table, through harder training, SMART technology and design ..."our design," said Hal, looking and sounding pleased.

And according to Coach Donaghue, the new sportswear design definitely helped during practice and workout sessions in boosting individual and team performance."

Everyone as a result was motivated to work harder and train smarter. All agreed on high fives, that the techies with a smattering of science, won on and off the field without even touching the ball.

"An awesome achievement," said Kyle. "Close to magic," said a smiling Jorge. "It sure is despite your disappearing act," said Hal, looking suspicious.

"Now that I've got to explain, but right now not sure if it was a real or imagined trip to an unknown planet somewhere out there in the galaxy," said an uncertain Jorge.

"Yeah right, so you may have found a genuine reason after all for your disappearing act at a crucial time on the project," said Hal.

"Yes, I may have been on another planet." "Jorge seriously, you need to get checked out, you're not making sense and its party time to celebrate our achievement and team the win," said Kyle. "I'm ready," said Hal. "Me too," said Jorge. "So what are we waiting for," said Kyle.

Jorge knew he needed he time to quietly and secretly process his so real planetary experience, but right now there was much too much happening on planet Earth to occupy his time.

So he felt no need to worry for the moment about being tracked again, as the code had been shortened at his insistence which puzzled the others. And thankfully they agreed after research findings proved code was not necessary would be replaced by sensors in the new batch of sportswear, after work in the lab was complete later next month.

Still, from time to time Jorge was left wondering about the bigger picture, and if he really had an outer planetary experience. As the weeks and months went by, there were some pointers to suggest this might have been the case. For starters, he could not locate his SMART watch or his brown leather jacket and there were tracks resembling a star opposite the ice cream parlour across the way.

Which is why Jorge couldn't forget or fully move on and continued to recount the experience to his family and friends. Along with the secret fear that next time the aliens might connect again and maybe kidnap his friends or family to obtain further information, spooked him.

His mother fretted to her friends that she feared Jorge may be on drugs, or have taken some drugs that permanently distort or damage the brain's chemistry. He was teased and made fun of by his friends, at the mention of other planets or the possibility life on distant planets.

His sister joked one morning as they left for college, that the band was the only element of cool left in his life. But Jorge wasn't concerned or such facts didn't even register.

The lady a couple of doors away who seemed to have three husbands or boyfriends who all adored her, met him one day on the way home and was all concerned," with utterances of "Jorge how are you, are you better" and how her niece thought he was cute. "Then there we hear all this stuff about other planets, shrinks, drugs", and the list of weird went on," said Jorge. "We were saying only the other day; thank god there are some regular, normal nice guys around like you." Jorge looked at her vacantly..."I'm sorry, Mrs...Ms Cody" "its Jo" – "of course Jo, I'm fine thanks; there are no drugs, shrinks, other planets or weird stuff. And if you don't mind, I'm in a hurry and have to get back to class," said Jorge. "Sure, I understand, we knew this was lies," said Mrs Cody."

"Then I get home one evening and hear my folks arguing, with Dad freaking out over the fact that his classified files may have been hacked, or that I somehow saw the contents, or maybe heard conversations with the control centre.

Not only that, but his managing director, Dr Ross, seemed to also have heard about Jorge's supposed trip to an unknown planet and joked, but at the same time, sounding nervous with "Larry, have we missed something in the search for life on other planets?"

And he continued, looking sceptical in an uncertain sounding tone with..."I mean, you guys are first rate and I know if there's something out there, you guys will turn it up, given the longer-term plan across the outer planets.

Let's all remember too, these are highly sensitive, classified, and confidential projects, which I will emphasise at the next briefing, along with the new security protocols. There is nothing yet to indicate our sensitive work-in progress data was stolen during that last mysterious outage. But my concern is that we haven't been able to identify the cause or trace those responsible, whether crackpots, professional hackers, or a nation state. Therefore, I have given our cyber and data protection people direct orders to take whatever steps are necessary to secure our data infrastructure," explained Dr Ross.

"So regardless of kids' talk about being accosted by aliens and taken to their planet, or other government wanting to steel our data or find something we missed, even rich folk with endless resources hoping to make some major discovery, and maybe they will. Let's keep focused on the project details and next phase, so we are on schedule."

"Sure thing Sir, that's our plan." "Good, I know we at the institute can depend on your findings as you guys are the best," said Dr Ross, still sounding nervous.

Mom then snapped after Dad recounted the conversation with his boss, Dr Ross. With "Larry, who cares about classified files, the people you talk to, what they heard, said, or your projects you work on. That's not the problem."

"Maybe you push Jorge too hard with science and mathematics, when you check in, just because there the subjects which are vital in your field," said Mom.

"You know honey, I just want Jorge to give science and mathematics his best shot now, he will always have time to change, even switch direction after college. Besides, he loves coding and all that technology stuff and that's where it's at for all his friends too, just look in the garage," said Dad.

"But there's so much pressure," said Mom. I would much rather Jorge be normal, getting on with day to day stuff, staying away from drugs and developing his natural talents - and maybe this is music, his band," said Mom.

"Oh for God sake honey, you cannot be serious, that's just a passing fad, a fun hobby, not something he will build a career in as it's so difficult to get a break without contacts and besides, there are no real music talents in our family," said Dad.

"My grandfather was a very fine musician actually," replied Mom. "Ok honey, but that was 100 years ago, now is a different time.

Besides, I don't think music, the sciences or mathematics are the issue or that we even have the answers to the problem. Which is why I think we should have him see someone," said Dad. In fact I will call Cal at the hospital, his nephew is a highly successful psychologist who will help see what the issues are and if they will impact his studies and life," said Dad.

"I would just like to establish a way for him to continue to be a normal, vibrant, fun person, just like the Jorge we know and love honey, without the influence of drugs, or the other negative vices that are out there. And then there's the constant pressure to study harder, get better grades and do more to excel," said Mom. Absolutely, that is vital, and important for him to realise, he has to work hard to achieve good results," insisted Dad.

"But you're right honey, I suppose we can ease off a little," said Dad, reluctantly agreeing, despite being stressed-out and anxious, as he left for yet another research trip in the desert, and if its drugs, uppers, downers, whatever, we'll find out too."

"Hey, don't I get a say in all this," asked Jorge, startling them both. "Jorge, your father and I are just concerned and you know we want the best for you."

His father's phone rang at the same time, as he was leaving, and he stepped into the study to take the call, but Jorge overheard some of the conversation and knew it was Justin, his father's friend and colleague on the research team. He overheard his Dad say "what memo, you're kidding, because I thought he sounded a little nervous during our last conversation as I left the office on Friday. So the plan is the same, great," said my Dad, sounding pleased as the conversation with Justin ended.

He said good bye, with the usual hug and instruction, "be a good boy for your mother Jorge, and then, "do me a favour, do not discuss aliens, other planets or ideas with anyone other than Gerard the Psychologist, and he's expecting to see you Thursday."

Despite Jorge's protestations and this being the third one, the first came highly recommended and expensive, insisted he saw himself in Jorge at seventeen, high on life, maybe over indulged on occasion and got confused, which Jorge insisted was not the case. The second suggested it was ambition and wanting to emulate his talented father, which was positive, but Jorge also disagreed with this analysis, even though he admired his father, and liked science, this was mostly because he found it easier than mathematics.

And when suggestions were made to try psychologist number three, Jorge, tried to avoid the appointment, insisting it was a waste of time and money as he was fine and really had forgotten events, but his father insisted.

Jorge did not want to argue, as he knew his dad was worried, and hoped the story about his son's trip to another planet with life, would permanently go away. "Sure," said Jorge hesitantly, I've almost forgotten anyway." Knowing it was the wrong time to mention the fact, that if his dream or extra terrestrial trip was for real, these aliens could view or steel whatever data was of interest from current or past projects, especially his research findings on extra terrestrial life.

So for now, it was yet another pointless trip to the shrink and all the looks, whispers, and giggles that went on as he showed up for class and practice. By now Jorge was flatly refusing or careful not to mention, other planets, even planet earth was off limits, despite requests from science magazines, TV networks, Radio stations, and other colleges.

Even though Jorge tried to forget, he could not fully discount the experience, and such interest from so many sources made it all the more difficult.

Then one evening Jorge was making his way back from band practice, he thought the reflection of the sun or maybe moon through the clouds above were unusually bright. Not only that, next time he looked, what seemed like a large round glass or silver object floated above the clouds, but hard to tell, as the evening sun blinded his vision.

When he got back home, he went to his den in the garage and as he switched on the computer. He could hear loud bleeping sounds in the background, and then sudden screeching sounds of cars and trucks coming to an instant stop, with panicked voices saying ..."did you see that"..."it's a spaceship" ..."it's real"..."kids, stay back"..."but dad"..."do what I say".

Jorge looked out the window, but his view was blocked by the trees and fence, he could see blue and silver rays reaching into the evening sky. And hear more startled sounding voices saying "the door of the spaceship is open", others uttering, "Oh my god aliens" ..."aliens have come to visit the neighbourhood". Then he heard a little girl say, "they look scary mommy".

Jorge's then knew for certain, his friends had returned, and heart started to pound with fear. The real or surreal moment that he worried about, sweated over and always dreaded, finally arrived, just as he was starting to forget events, even avoid the conversation, and he buried his face in his hands helplessly, trying to figure out what he would do.

His phone rang, it was Louilla about the movies. "Lou, you cannot believe it." "Believe what Jorge, are you ok ... you sound weird." "I...the aliens from space have arrived." Jorge, why can't you just be normal - I thought you said you had forgotten this stuff," said Louilla. "I have ...I mean I did, but its real now," said an overwhelmed sounding Jorge. With that, the phone went dead and he was left with "hello ...hello."

He raced out to the garden and saw Starstarz and Prajkery at the front door. Then heard his Mom scream and after in a panicked voice said "honey are you ok" as dad had collapsed. Starstarz suggested he was probably a little shocked seeing folk he spent almost a lifetime looking for, on his doorstep.

"Ah there you are Jorge, we came to return your replacement SMART watch, we destroyed, which will function in exactly the same way, and this souvenir bracelet from your trip to our planet, oh and you ... or we also forgot your jacket that time, with the rush to get you back safely. We are very sorry you had to leave so quickly," said Starstarz. "It's ok; you didn't have to stuttered," Jorge in amazement, "but thanks."

"Jorge, honey," whimpered Mom looking shocked at this point and holding on to the door ledge for support. "Mom its ok," said an even more shocked Jorge.

"How did you find me this time – I mean I disabled the code?" asked a frightened Jorge.

At that same moment, Kyle and Hal burst through the front gate, their bikes coming to an instant screeching stop, with "man – you were right, you are not crazy" and then their voices got quieter and trailed off, when they saw Starstarz and Prajkery.

Jorge could still hear the emergency services and extra police cars zooming in the background as Starstarz continued saying how "the Gods were angry and viewed the last mission as unauthorized and off limits. Even though we followed protocol, acted fairly, and no one was injured. Celest saved the day, as her project and efforts to get the real facts impressed her father, the higher and most senior God, Arkadykte, ensuring a future seat on the panel and all the advantages associated with such a powerful role.

But unfortunately, we have been ordered to abort all further research, data gathering and fact-finding missions to planet Earth, as the Gods and the higher panel have decided they now have all the information and resources required. Our planet is light years ahead of planet Earth as our systems and processes are more advanced and at the necessary level to ensure our planets safety and long-term security.

Besides, the senior God does not want his daughter Celest getting any further ideas about exploration trips to Earth when she graduates next year, and felt it best we focus on strengthening our own internal security systems to prevent intruders and invasions from other planets.

Therefore, I am returning the files we put together and other data we availed of including your father's research and tireless work on locating life on other planets," said Starstarz.

Jorge could see police pulling up in the background and two helicopters overhead. About a dozen dark blue giant robots with what looked like automatic rifles poured out of the pyramid shaped structure, with a loudspeaker saying "please do not approach, we mean you no harm. We just came to deliver something Jorge forgot when he visited our planet earlier".

With that, Starstarz held out her hand, "so Jorge our work is now done, thank you and goodbye." Jorge at this point was stunned. Starstarz ventured again, "Its ok Jorge ...are you ok Jorge – you understand, you are very white? Don't be frightened, we mean you no harm, you know this from our earlier meeting." "We are a peaceful force," said the other alien Prajkery who moved closer to Starstarz. "Sure...I...absolutely," agreed an uncertain and shocked Jorge, finding it difficult to react or respond to events.

"Hurry, we must leave now," instructed Starstarz, as she looked at the read alarm on her wrist band, pressed a dial and ordered "dim the lights and move to invisible."
Then in instant, Starstarz pulled what looked like a sword and moved away backward. The Robots then ushered them into the space ship, and followed behind.

A couple of seconds later they were in the clouds, with just an intermittent flicker of blue and silver light sparkling through, as they vanished from view into the evening sky. Kyle and Hal were awe struck, standing transfixed, in total shock, as they watched the spaceship rise into the evening sky and then disappear in an instant.

Leaving everyone in the neighbourhood shocked, surrounded by all the usual security, TV, Radio Stations, Newspapers pouring in with the ambulance also clamouring to reach Jorge's house as his dad had still not regained consciousness.

As the movie ended, Jorge was still part of the ongoing project and deemed an expert on outer space and alien life. Kyle was the technology specialist, Hal the scientist and Jorge was planning a career as an Astrophysicist, deciding he would have to keep one eye on planet earth activities and the other for sightings of his friends from unknown planets beyond the stars.

12

SUMMER HOLIDAYS

Rebecca is going to France in the summer to improve her language skills and Adrianna has decided to go along also. They will first arrive in Belgium and then travel onwards by train to Luxemburg and France.

The girls will spend four weeks in France, two weeks attending classes to improve their language skills, and afterwards help friends in their vineyard, during the busy harvesting season in late summer and autumn.

Adrianna told Rebecca about her lesson on vineyard activity also know as viticulture. One evening as she was having a glass of wine with some colleagues from work, and was sitting next to Christopher, who impressed everyone with his expertise on best seasons wine to select from the wine list.

The conversation then continued about favourite wines, prize-winning local wines and the very best wines on the shelf right now. Adrianna told how Christopher she would be spending some time helping friends in their vineyard during the busy summer harvesting season.

"You must remember, every month is busy in the vineyard Adrianna, from the time the earliest shoots appear in early spring until the vines are dormant in December," explained Christopher.

"Really," said Adrianna – "yes," said Christopher. "I know this because we lived beside a vineyard until I was 10 years old. Even in December, the dormant vines are pruned to ensure a stronger and healthier re-growth. And there may also be some wine tasting in December and around New Year.

Work in the vineyard starts over again when the vines wake up in February and March. The young vines are fastened to wire that runs alongside each row of vines.

April, and in fact all through spring, favourable weather conditions are so important. The growers are hoping there will be no frost, or extreme cold and rain, which damage and reduce the crop yield, and oftentimes wipe out the entire crop in some regions.

When my brother and I were little, I remember we used to go and play in the windmill at the vineyard. The windmill was built to keep the air circulating round the vineyard to prevent frost," explained Christopher.

"Uncertain weather conditions have become more frequent in recent times, with sudden storms, torrential rain and higher temperatures, now attributed to global warming."

"By May and definitely June, the vines are laden with budding green grapes and some are pruned back to ensure a strong healthy crop, leaving just two or three branches per vine. The vines are fastened again at a higher point to the wire to allow maximum sunshine for grapes to ripen. Fresh air and irrigation are also important at this time too.

Vineyard activity is highly regulated and there are strict rules for growing, harvesting during the production process, and afterwards for bottling and labelling of the wines for sale. And any unexpected disturbances during the growing period, will damage the grape crop and reduce yield.

I know this because we lived very close to a large vineyard. On my 8th birthday, I got a puppy called Jewels. One evening after school as we were playing close to the vineyard, a cat appeared. Jewels saw the cat that ran through the vineyard to escape and Jewels chased after through row after row of vines, disturbing some, damaging others as they fell to the ground, and the fun didn't stop there," said Christopher.

"Jewles continued to race after the cat to the other side of the road, through a large open gate and up a long tree lined driveway, across the lawn of a huge chateau and onto a movie set. I followed behind on my bike, trying hard to catch up, shouting "Jewels come back, stop. As I raced across the lawn towards the trees, I heard startled voices through trees on the other side of the lawn shouting...did you see that?" What was that? What is going on"...with other loud voices shouting, "stop", "stop right there!! "Cut!"

A table of champagne and glasses, bowls of fruit, various meat platters, biscuits and a cheese board were drawn to the floor, as the cat ran under the table followed by Jewels who got caught in the table covering. "What is going on, where is security, what do I pay you guys for," said a tall man dressed in white, wearing a straw boater hat. At that point, about three guys in black with dark glasses appeared from nowhere and joined the chase. "Hey little fella, stop". There were other voices repeating, "stop" and "he's now close to the pool".

I knew we were in big trouble and was terrified. Jewels continued racing after the dam cat, slipped or more like slid across the wet tiles by the pool and ended up in the water frantically splashing around. To the alarm of others on sun loungers at the far side of the pool and to my great shock, I honestly thought he was going to drowned. As he panted and paddled, frantically trying to escape. Frightening and amusing the children who were also splashing around in the pool on inflatable water duck.

At that point I was surrounded by the guys in black with what seemed like a hundred questions to answer," said Christopher. "We better remove our uninvited guest from the pool," said another as Jewels continued to splash around in the shallow part. As he came closer to the edge of the pool, he started to crawl up the steps to the loud laughs and amusement of the children, who were at this point, ordered from the pool and were watching from the decking area.

Just then a really tall man with a moustache approached with two others behind in vexed voices, one throwing his hands up into the air saying it's probably as good as what we have been trying to get all day! "Young man, why did you come on to private property...do you know what happens to naughty little people like you and your wild puppy. I remember almost starting to cry with fear, as the man looked so serious and scary," recounted Christopher.

"Sir...Your cat was"..."was what young man," asked the infuriated tall man with the moustache. As he moved closer, I pointed across at the same time in the direction of the vineyard..."the cat, it was the cat", was all I could utter with fear," said Christopher. Jamie my brother then appeared... the scary man Harold turned around staring blankly at my brother frightening him also.

"Christopher, papa is looking for you... He is very angry," his eyes then darting back to Harold, who stood as if frozen with his arms folded, asked in an angry voice..."who...I mean where is your papa"? At that moment, his bleep or sort of alarm sounded on his phone. Answering it while keeping his eyes on us, he snapped "will be right there."

A tall glamorous woman then appeared holding the cat and stroking it at the same time...Saying "Harold...it's the darn cat, his dog seemingly followed our cat," said the woman. "But why are they here on our lawn ...the movie set...the overturned table of refreshments, broken glasses of Champaign...for the barbecue, all in a mess on the lawn. There are questions, but frankly young man I don't have time for this distraction, or the fact that you and our cat or whoever, turned my movie world upside down in an instant.

Darling can you sort this out the studio people have arrived... I must get back... we've already lost enough of time and this is an interruption I could do without," said Harold impatiently.

Next thing my father arrived and Jewels ran over to him, his lead dragging on the ground, pausing to shake himself dry at the same time.

178

"What happened," asked my father. "Its Erika...nice to meet you," said the woman to my father, "he then became less anxious," said Christopher. "I think my cat crossed paths with your dog and the end result was a disrupted movie set," said Erica.

"Papa was so angry even though everyone was ok - well after the small interrogation by the guys in black, at the sudden breach of security, and the disruption caused to the movie set at the chateau. And Mr Mendoza in the vineyard still had to be appeased. Papa went by that evening and he was grumbling, and startled at the same time, over the damage done. Along with the extra effort and time required to fix or remove the damaged vines, after what he called 'the stampede' through the vineyard. And how it cannot happen again, his anxiety communicated by his startled expression - and papa of course assured him it would not.

But after that incident, Mr Mendoza viewed my brother and I with suspicion and studied our moves from the distance, especially if we were close to the vineyard, where he was frequently seen. A couple of days later and to our utter amazement, the Director wanted to re-create the scene for their movie called 'Suspect and Suspense'. They liked the instantaneous appearance of Jewels chasing after the cat in the storyline, leading to the discovery of key suspects and wanted to get some more general shots to edit him into the scene," said Christopher.

"That is magic, so you caused them to rewrite the script or part of the story and then got to be a movie star for the day," said Adrianna. "Well not quite. Jewels did, because don't forget he had raced ahead and onto the movie set, was caught on camera and almost in the pool when I arrived. As I couldn't ride my bike across the lawn, but we got to see activity on a real movie set and that was cool," said Christopher.

"Afterwards when we were on school vacation, we got to use the pool, tennis court and basketball court of the famous director's chateau," said Christopher.

July and August are busy months in the vineyard, and cellar too as the vines are heavy with grapes and are fastened more securely to wire running along-side to   allow air to circulate ensuring healthy vines so grapes don't rot.

Wine in the cellars is bottled at this time also, to make way for the new harvest.

Harvesting time depends on the weather, but usually starts from early to mid August in some regions through to September and October when the grapes are fully ripe for picking by hand or with machines.

Once the grapes are picked, they are then crushed lightly and placed in huge vats to ferment. Red grapes ferment with their skins intact, this gives red wine its rich colour. After a couple of days the White wine is skimmed to separate it from its skin and stored in metal vats, in order to continue the fermenting process. Yeast is often used in the fermenting process; this turns the wine juice into ethanol alcohol. Some organic producers prefer not to use a fermenting agent.

In November, the grapes may be stirred in their vats, to enhance the flavour and the vineyard is cleared and tidied up. "I was helping out that November in the Cellar, and wait for this. A huge limo drove up outside, out gets the chauffeur and drops in four cream gold embossed envelopes with guess what," said Christopher. "An invitation to a party," guessed Adrianna." "Actually an invitation to a movie premiere which was awesome," said Christopher. I'm actually still friends with the director's two sons, Jacques and Fabian."

"Mr Mendoza was asked to supply as much wine as possible from his cellar for the premiere and after party. And his pre-Christmas wine-tasting event resulted in immediate sell-out orders for new season's wines.

The grape type gives the wine its name, but depending on regulation and there are so many, some growers will also state the name of the chateau, particularly if a famous producer in the region," said Christopher. "I feel like an expert," said Adrianna. "I'm sure you will learn much more when you are there. As things change and every region is different. Some folk are going back to basics doing most of the harvesting manually to ensure highest quality organic vintage," said Christopher.

"How very interesting," said Rebecca. "It's true, everything depends on the weather and location," said Adrianna.

"Exactly like our vacation," said Rebecca. "Well similar," said Adrianna. "The location according to Christopher is important, as grapes grown in vineyards close to the ocean will produce a different flavoured wine to those grown further inland or in varied climatic conditions and the soil too determines the quality and flavour of the wine," explained Adrianna.

The girls are already excited and it's still only November. They just have now to work out the journey plans, the route they will take and how long they will stay in each place. After this budget to cover travel costs, thought Adrianna.

Rebecca's friend Fabio suggested they book as soon as possible and get the necessary documentation required when taking along the two puppies. "We will have to take Buddy and Brett to the vet to get necessary injections and microchips required to take the puppies out of the country," said Adrianna.

HOLIDAY PLANS AND JOURNEY DETAILS

"Rebecca, once you have booked your language lessons at the school in France and have agreed the dates, let me know as I will also book my programme. We then have to plan for the next four weeks," said Adrianna.

After spending time helping in the vineyard, we could continue south to visit the warm, sunny costal region and explore the beautiful surrounds before journeying over the Pyrenees into Spain. Then travel northwards to Italy to explore some historic towns, villages and vineyards along the way and view the amazing renaissance art and architecture.

We will continue the journey northwards to the point where the Rhine River starts - almost as stream from a glacier in the Swiss Alps. Maybe even visit Europe's highest vineyard and wine cellars, if reasonably close by while in Switzerland.

Visit the beautiful lake Constance where the Rhine River cascades from the Alps as it journeys North West through Europe, providing a rich source of drinking water to regions along its path. A key commercial trade, route since Roman times, where ships, barges and boats, transport oil, gas, coal and grain to towns and cities along its waterways.

"Fabio said the Alpine route can be treacherous due to the very busy narrow roads, most of which are at high altitude," said Rebecca. A little like our own country," laughed Adrianna with the narrow roads but without the altitude problem."

"Well at least there won't be snow or ice in the Alps at this time of year and the scenery will be majestic and the views breathtaking.

Besides I have driven in Europe before and I was fine. I think the SUV that the travel agent suggested will be perfect, as it's very spacious and comfortable especially on a long journey with Brett, Buddy and the luggage," said Rebecca.

They agreed to follow the path of the Rhine River into Germany's Bavaria as it journey through woodlands, valleys, picturesque fairy-tale villages and magical castles.

"We will have to stop and visit some of those ancient castles originally built as early day fortresses, with strategic military significance on the hilltops and mountains, to protect the surrounding village inhabitants from marauding armies that travelled the Rhine River. According to the guidebook, some castles were built as summer retreats, others as official residences for archbishops, European Royal families and gatekeepers of the region and those castles reminded Adrianna of a story she heard when she was a little girl, about a boy called Arden.

"One day after school, when out walking in the woods, Arden climbed a giant oak tree trying to reach some acorns for his schools nature table.

He remembered seeing some golden coloured acorns higher up in the tall tree, but as he got closer he couldn't move and felt scared. Then suddenly as if by magic, he was transported to a world beyond and into what seemed like a deep valley at first in a strange distant land surrounded by golden clouds.

Arden journeyed through the valley and forest, vineyards, olive groves, lavender, sunflower and wheat fields, hoping to find some sign of life, in what appeared like a magical kingdom, with a huge rainbow sparkling overhead as if marking its territory or a treasure beyond.

He passed little cottages with colourful gardens, but everyone inside them seemed to disappear behind curtains. Then he came to a school and saw little elf-like children playing outside, they ran for cover as soon as they saw this stranger in their mist. Why is everyone so scared thought Arden, surely they must know I mean them no harm.

In the distance beyond, he could see a huge mountain and at the top of the mountain was a castle. He could also see a long winding river flow down the mountain to a lake in the valley. As evening turned to night, the castle lights in the distance sparkled in the moonlight.

As he journeyed on, he came to a bridge and was starting to feel tired and weary. He could hear the most beautiful music in the distance, which sounded like a lullaby.

Arden sat down on a bench under a tall willow tree and started to wonder where the music was coming from as he rested.

Feeling weary after his long journey he went off to sleep to the sound of bells chiming and lutes and harps playing the sweetest music ever. The genie appeared to Arden, saying how she had found his 'rainy day wish', for an adventure to a new and unknown world, and it had been granted.

The next sound he heard was a loud ringing in his ear and voices saying "wake up laddie." When Arden opened his eyes, he was surrounded by men in bright costumes with shields, three standing over him, one shouted "get up lad, who are you." "I am Arden Sir." "What are you doing here and where have you come from." But before Arden could answer, the King cut in. "Did Dadelious send you to spy on his neighbour?

"Who is Dadel.iou..s," asked Arden, struggling to pronounce the name. Laddie he is a feared, cunning and ruthless ruler to the south of Alislam and Tibilis is his son.

"There's a mistake," said Arden... "There is no mistake unless it's your mistake laddie," said the furious red-faced King. "I will not be tricked again do you hear me? Where are you from lad"? "My village by the river and the old oak trees, I then journeyed in the mist through the valley then suddenly I arrived here.
I was lost and trying to find my way back, then stopped to rest and fell asleep after the long journey through the valley and forest," replied Arden.

"Ah that's why there was such silence and sneaking around. I knew something was wrong; there was an intruder in our midst," said the King.

"Well you have entered the world beyond, this is my domain. This is Alislam, I am King of Alislam, and this is my hunting army. We do not like strangers in Alislam." So the King instructed his men who were dressed in eleven-like costumes to take Arden to the cellar.

"You will be my prisoner until I can decide what best what to do you lad. We must find out for real who this intruder is and where his people are," said the king.

186

"Many Kingdoms were lost through extravagance and carelessness in dealing with the enemy, do you hear me - this will not happen in my Kingdom. More importantly, I have to decide if he is here by accident or here to spy on our army's plans, even steel our Kingdom treasures and secrets for the despicable Dadelious. Whose cunning almost worked until he lost the dual to take half my army?

"I get angry when I am happy and angry when I am sad, when I sing and when I dance at the mention of Dadelious, his people, his puppets or his plans. And intruders, or spies sent on his behalf will have no chance at all when captured. So let's hope you are not part of Dadelious deceitful plan for your own sake Laddie. As the outcome of course will also depend on how angry I am at the time, but will not be pleasant for either of you. Do you hear me boy? "Yes Sir I hear you but"…and before Arden could finish speaking, the King cut in "I want to banish Dadelious from my Kingdom, as he is just watching and waiting for any chance to pounce on my treasures, my army, and my precious kingdom of Alislam – so enough," shouted the red faced angry King.

Next thing, the King was interrupted by a sweet girl, saying, "pa pa, the deer got away." "Octavia, Octavia, where are you going"? "We were hunting and I missed my shot, the deer got away, can I try again this afternoon, as the games are only two weeks away."

"You have archery practice in this afternoon", said a voice in the background. Do you hear your mother, my Queen, darling, whatever makes you happy - let us return to the castle and see what is best," said the softer sounding King.

So the King, Queen with his daughter Octavia surrounded by their army went back to the castle. They went over a wide drawbridge leading across the river, then through arches to the main entrance of the castle grounds. As they arrived everything was formal with a flurry of activity from guardsmen. Your Majesty, two governors have arrived to discuss matters of state and unusual sightings from the castle wall along the river.

Arden was in awe as he looked around the huge courtyard. The king spoke with two guardsmen who then lead him through a long gallery with huge portraits covering the walls; further on as the door was open, he could see a library with a desk, and round shaped room with piano, huge mirrors and comfortable seating. Arden was put in a cellar to the side off the large dining room, but could see through a small breaking in the wall across the room where two throne like chairs stood on a raised platform at the top.

Behind the chairs was a huge tapestry that hung from beams in the high ceiling to the floor. There was a huge lifelike eagle on the tapestry surrounded by two gold swords entwined by roses.

Arden now guessed why everyone was silent and rushed behind their curtains when they saw him as he journeyed through the valley and woodlands trying to find life in this mysterious kingdom of Alislam. Everyone was afraid for intruders as they were not welcome and would be punished by the King. Arden was afraid and confused as if awakening from a bad dream. How did I get here, and how am I going to get back to my village. He had totally forgotten about his 'rainy day wish' to the genie, made with friends during a cold, dark winter evening, and couldn't recall how he arrived in such a strange kingdom.

Suddenly he heard steps coming towards the door of the cellar, a chunky key turned, in marched two guards and threw a selection of clothes on the bench to the side by the wall. The second guard left a plate of what looked like stew, but smelled like fish, and a plate of bread, honey and milk.

"My lady ordered this for you." "Oh," said the Arden, "I am grateful, and please pass on my appreciation and thanks. But when can I go home? "Don't you think that is being ungracious – the King has instructed you be detained until he is certain he knows who you are and where you are from. Only then can you be on your way. In the meantime, they want you to join them in archery, and other sports ahead of the forthcoming annual kingdom games. You may be invited to participate, if you demonstrate merit during practice," said the guardsman. "But I"… "No buts" snapped the guardsman, "finish your food as you will need strength and stamina."

"The games will take place inside the castle walls to the east in the arena. It's a big occasion for the kingdom, as friend and foe gather to show off their skills. Winners are granted prestigious titles and positions of power in the army and governing council of the kingdom. Our king loves winners, there is a special place in his heart and world for winners laddie, especially if one of his own wins. They are taken care of for life, given their own castle or one strategically located with

189

land and a mini-army, so there is a lot at stake for everyone laddie," explained the guardsman.

"But surely those rules will not apply to me, besides; I am not from the Kingdom of Alislam or territories beyond," replied Arden. "The only games I have ever competed in are on our schools sports day and I did win a medal for rowing last year also."

"Winners are of interest to the King no matter where they are from and existing leaders compete to appoint the strongest warriors from the winners."

Adrianna remembered from the story, that Arden showed skill beyond his youthful freshness and excelled in all sports especially archery. The king was impressed, even though it was earlier agreed he would not enter in the forthcoming games. But with some practice, he would be more than able to participate in later competitions.

The King appointed tutors to instruct and educate Arden who was showing great promise and worked hard to perfect his sporting and competitive skills as well as his music, mathematics and classical studies.

Arden became a skilful apprentice, and was improving with every passing month. He was also growing taller with piercing blue eyes and blonde hair that fell loosely around his ears. The King got suspicious on many occasions when no trace of Arden's people could be found.

They heard news of a plague in faraway lands, inhabitants fleeing to join enemy armies and to work on development projects. So the King had the enemy and surrounding kingdoms watched with eagle-eyes for irregular movements.

All that turned up from the exercise was some poachers sailing the river by night to fish and were apprehended and punished accordingly. An outcome that disappointed the King who had hoped for some news regarding enemy moves, plans and development projects.

Adrianna recalled the stories happy ending, that saw Arden not only win a number of competitions at the games, but also become a skilful soldier and subsequently was given his own army, castle and watch tower. His troops saw off a number of threats and challenges to the Kingdom of Alislam not least from Hevron, leader of the mighty kingdom of Seldsbown, to the north, whom Octavia, the kings daughter eventually married. The happy ever part eventually came through too for Arden, when he won the hand of the queen's cousin Matilda from the kingdom of Hadrian.

Hadrian was a bitter enemy until the queen wed the king, and brought about a thaw in relations, but Hadrian still posed a distant threat to Alisalm, a threat the king was well aware of and prepared for.

Arden's marriage had the approval of the mighty king and queen, especially after his discovery of new lands and a kingdom much bigger than Alislam, where he eventually held a senior governing position and was also favoured by the Queen as a future ruler of Alislam.

The Queen had started to grow tired of what she called the king's imagined enemies. She knew from her own sources too that there was no immediate or future threat of war to the kingdom and managed to garner more influence and power than the king, who at times was given to bouts of depression, madness and delirium.

While old enemies and other powers of perceived threat were busy consolidating power, developing the arts and architecture and forging new economic partnerships to compete with counterparts in other kingdoms. "This is how to govern a kingdom and what I want for our kingdom," said the Queen to the king, after another pointless night watching for imagined enemies, while others were embarking on voyages of discovery to new lands and forging strong trading ties.

"I want Arden as our governor," announced the Queen. "After all, he is an accomplished soldier, army officer, ambitious and successful too, someone that will make our Kingdom great again."

"I have ordered plans for his castle and fortress with private apartments my dear," replied the king calmly, where he will have the position of governor." The castle will stand overlooking the kingdom on a solid Moat, surrounded by a reinforced Bailey and a Keep to the north by the inner wall. The outer walls will have eight Turrets to ensure adequate defence in the event of attack from hostile forces.

The drawbridge leading to the main entrance is optional and useful especially in times of strife, but this is Arden decision. The queen smiled and ordered the best vintage wine to celebrate such unexpected good news.

Arden work up startled and exhausted but pleased to be in the real world, after a day rehearsing the lines for his medieval play, that seemed even better in his dreams.

"God I can't remember how long ago I heard that story. Maybe it's the reason castles have always fascinated me," said Adrianna, "with the possibility of a mysterious and magical story within. And the reasons I am always so drawn to explore and discover the story behind such imposing stone structures, built to protect ruling dynasties of a bygone era. Often set in impossible locations on islands, highlands, lakes and in forests, or in this case, along a strategic commercial river passage.

"My history lessons were enough to stem the curiosity and fascination with castles" said Rebecca, "as they were always linked to 'had to know dates', denoting a significant siege, power struggle or historic battles to ward off enemy invasions and perilous rule of our land. In fact, my history class was full of such dates and events."

"You are right, and this time we can walk into history, as we travel onwards, as there are so many splendid castles still there today overlooking the great river Rhine, whose free flowing waters define the spirit and character of modern day Europe. A river steeped in folklore and celebrated through song and stories.

Small and large boats, tug boats, barges and ships journey daily on this busy inland waterway to commercial ports and trading points along the great River Rhine," said Adrianna.

"I think this part of our trip will be more exciting and adventurous than the inward journey, as there is so much to see," exclaimed Rebecca. "We could take a boat trip on the river Rhine or cycle along its bank and maybe stop for a picnic, relax and savour the surrounds, hike in the Black forest.

From there, cross the border into the Netherlands and time permitting, explore some more before the homebound journey via Belgium, leaving little time before our mid-day departure. There is so much to do in the meantime and hopefully lots of fun and adventure ahead," said Rebecca.

SUMMER ESSENTIALS and HOLIDAY CHECKLIST

"I will have to buy some summer clothes and holiday accessories," exclaimed Adrianna. "You don't want to over-pack and take too much," said Rebecca. "My rule is, just pack light as there will be less to carry and if you need additional stuff, you can always buy it locally."

"The weather will be very warm most days so I will just need a couple pairs of light cotton trousers, some shorts, two or three cotton dresses and some jeans for the not so warm days, or when helping out in the vineyard," said Rebecca.

"I am taking my hiking boots along anyway," said Adrianna. "And I would never forget my sunglasses along with the even more essential high protection sun cream lotion and the dreaded insect repellent, as the mosquitoes start to bite especially in the cool evening air."

"I have the perfect essential guidebook with maps and useful information for most areas on our journey route, so I don't think it's necessary to buy another one Adrianna and the travel agents will also include some additional details," said Rebecca.

"A list with an accompanying trip outline and journey details is the best way to ensure everything is organised and nothing is forgotten, as the list will include the necessary travel essential action points," said Adrianna.

"I agree. The travel agents will give us train timetables and a more specific road map, with distance and length of time between locations," said Rebecca.

THE LIST

1. *Book the language school in France*
2. *Driving licence/ Passports – ensure current*
3. *Book the return flights via the travel agents*
4. *Book the SUV utility vehicle to collect in Switzerland return in Belgium.*
5. *Take Buddy and Brett to the vet for the necessary shots and microchip to meet national /EU travel regulations.*
6. *Make Train reservations*
7. *Book Accommodation on route to Spain, France, Italy and Switzerland.*

TRIP OUTLINE

Outward journey

- *Belgium*
- *France Study language and Vineyard*
- *Spain, the Pyrenees*

Return journey

- *Alps —Italian and Swiss — start of the River Rhine*
- *France, Language school and Vineyards*
- *Germany on Rhine River path and Black Forest*
- *Netherlands, Northern Renaissance art and architecture*

Luggage and Holiday essentials to pack:

1. *Summer essentials, insect repellent, Sunscreen, travel size cosmetic essentials.*
2. *Travel guide and French, Spanish and German language phrase books*
3. *Camera, sunglasses, hiking boots, sun hat and first aid kit.*
4. *3 pairs of summer pants, 3 pairs of shorts, 3 tee-shirts, 2 cotton dresses, 2   cardigans, 2 jumpers 1 pair of Jeans, 2 pairs of canvass shoes. 2 light jackets/ one waterproof jacket.*

13
STORIES OF ADVENTURE, DISCOVERY AND DREAMS

Adrianna just came back from a final briefing for the forthcoming conference and road show event for her boss, Edwin. Delighted with progress and planning as the entire programme was now organised including all key note speakers for the event.

Edwin will first go to office locations in China with a full agenda of meetings and then travels to the Koreas and Japan where he will deliver keynote speeches that have been painstakingly worked on and rehearsed.

Asia seems magical especially in springtime with beautiful tree blossom and snow-capped mountains. There are so many interesting sights and delights to savour according Sheria, who spent some time in various locations with work, and said Asia was the perfect place to explore new and different cultures.

Oh, I have to stop dreaming! God what time is it? Suddenly startled by an alarm on her mobile phone, signifying another task for next Mondays deadline.
Right now, I need to ensure the draft climate report is on Edwin's desk, the videoconference is on track, and there are no further questions before heading home.
Then I will take Buddy and Brett for their walk, despite the pouring rain as they have not been out much this week. I really should stop by

the library at the University on the way home, but I will do this at lunch time tomorrow, so I can get the relevant material to complete the project, and maybe even get a couple of travel guides too.

Later on that evening, Adrianna caught up with a couple of friends from college who travelled to some amazing locations around the world and on hearing their stories of adventure, mentioned her cultural and lifestyle trip idea with Buddy and Perry the poodle.

Maybe travel to Ecuador in South America and see the efforts being made to combat the impact of global warming with extensive tree planting. "That's like China, where they have an annual tree-planting day in March," said Jake.

"That's interesting, as they are also preventing further logging of trees in the Amazon Rain forest too," said Justine. Who then recounted the time she and Frank visited South America as part of their research and exploration trip to the Amazon tropical rain forest. "An adventure that ended with us falling down a ravine, getting lost, having a reasonably close encounter with a cougar and finally, being rescued by some Amazonian Rainforest natives," said Justine, as she continued to recount details of the adventure.

"After visiting Machu Picchu, we then journeyed onwards for a four day trip through the Amazon rainforest. There were about twelve to fourteen in our group and after breakfast on day four, after we moved from base camp, when I suddenly realised I had left my camera behind," recounted Justine. "So Frank and I quickly rushed back to see if we could locate it. As we passed a giant tree, a huge cat with wild eyes jumped onto our path. We were totally scared and changed direction quickly to somehow escape or lose the reasonably huge beast. We were racing quickly and the cat was also following in our direction, but he jumped on to some rocks above the tree, at the same time alarming the surrounding wildlife habitat. As about a dozen multi-coloured birds flew from the tall monkey-puzzle trees.

We then could hear more rustling movement in the understory vegetation among the vines, lianas and cecropia trees, and thought the cat may be close. So we decided to move on to the grassy patch, when suddenly some loose rocks gave way, and we both slipped down a steep incline or ravine towards a woodland area in a valley, grazing our faces and bruising our legs and arms. As we sat there in shock examining our wounds, we could see the cat on the tall rocks above, pacing back and forth, as if figuring out how to reach us, which sent tremors through us both. While still shaken after our sudden descent, and stressed too, as we were now out of range, out of sight of our group, and lost in the tropical rain forest," said Justine.

Frank didn't think we were too far away, I disagreed said Justine. Besides, at this point I was totally scared, but tried to be brave, as the sweltering sun started to burn down, we continued cautiously through the dense rainforest and came to a lake. I can see why most folks travel by river in the tropical rainforest," said Justine. "That doesn't matter at this point as we don't have a boat and we are lost," replied Frank. "So after checking the ground to avoid any further unwelcome encounters with any of the hundreds of reptiles and insect species that populate the rainforest, we sat on some rocks by the lake, to discuss our next move," recounted Justine.

"All I have is this mobile phone, with no signal, oh, I almost forgot, as he removed the small sized rucksack from his back, and this guidebook for South America. Let's see if there are any maps," said Frank.

He went to the section 'your Amazon Rainforest adventure'. "For god sake," I snapped anxiously, this is hardly an adventure Frank." "Well maybe more like an adventure unfolding." "You mean nightmare," said Justine nervously. "And it's unlikely a solution will emerge in that guide book."

"Stay calm," said Frank – "right now we are a little off course and hopefully lost the cat, which I think is a young Cougar." "What did you just say? I think it's a cougar," said Frank. "At that point, I was almost ventilating with fear, as I knew they could eat you alive," recounted Justine. Frank said it was the Jaguar we needed to most worry about meeting, as that animal was known as 'he who kills in one leap and is revered by the god even in afterlife'.

"Then shortly after, as Frank continued to study the guidebook, I could hear a sudden rustling in the bushes behind. "What's was that," I whispered. "Where," said Frank, "I thought I heard a rustling movement," said Justine. "It's probably the trees," said Frank – "maybe it's that cat again," said Justine.

Frank put down the guidebook and as we both stood up; strangely decorated tribal natives, with bow and arrows, suddenly surrounded us. "Stay calm," said Frank softly.

The tribal warriors spoke loudly in their own language, as if calling others from the forest behind, and were pointing towards us both at the same time. I was absolutely frozen with fear, and almost starting to cry," said Justine, as I remembered seeing a movie when younger, where such tribes captured and then carried out ritual ceremonies involving burning their captives as offerings to their Gods.

Frank could feel his heart pounding, but also tried to stay calm. We were ushered along the lake that veered left, onto a stony track, past some huts similar to those we stayed in the previous nights. Two tribal natives went ahead and there were two behind us," said Justine.

"I don't think they are hostile or mean any harm," whispered Frank "as they haven't used force, just gestured for us to move as directed, even though we are more or less surrounded and couldn't escape."

"Don't forget, a couple more from what I could see raced on ahead, probably to warn the others of the intruders in their mist, or maybe dinner, I whispered fearfully," said Justine.

"After about thirty minutes trekking through dense forest, pausing only to take a sip of water from a bottle that Frank luckily had in his rucksack. We continued along the stony path by a waterway, in the sweltering mid-day heat, that lead to a sudden clearing, from where we could see the pier, movement and life in the distance. With people milling around a large boat moored close by, and others getting off a coach. Frank and I held hands and breathed a huge sigh of relief; we would not die just yet, regardless of how lost we were.

As we got closer, we could see our group had assembled and Surri the leader was speaking to police officers. As we approached, she greeted us and then thanked the native tribal folk. Two police officers spoke with them briefly before they headed back by the lake towards the forest again.

"Frank and I joined our group as they embarked the river cruiser, for the final part of our journey. I had forgotten my expensive camera along with the amazing pictures and videos taken on the trip, and didn't care at that point if I never saw another one," said Justine.

"I cannot begin to tell you how delighted we both were to be on that boat regardless of how totally magical and amazing the previous three days were in the tropical Amazon Rainforest.

As the last couple of hours were totally terrifying and mostly of my own making," admitted Justine "because I should never have left the group to go back through dense forest to locate a camera, even though it seemed only five minutes away," said Justine.

"A scary story, but a kind of adventure too," said Adrianna, "as you had an off track view of the rainforest." "That's true," said Justine "but even if we were off track, we were much too scared to enjoy the getting lost adventure. In fact we were terrified of being bitten by a snake or other venomous reptiles that inhabit the dense rainforest, especially given the fact that approximately 35% of the worlds known wildlife species live in the Amazon rainforest." "You guys were very lucky to escape the wild cat or cougar," said Adrianna. "I know," said Justine.

"I thought I saw a giant otter further along the lake shore, but forgot to mention it to Frank, as the native tribal people appeared at the same time, so as you can imagine, I was a little distracted. If honest, the only other fear I had was of meeting or getting too close to an anaconda or their friends.

You really have to visit to appreciate the beauty of the tropical rainforest," said Justine. "It's already on my travel wish-list," replied Adrianna.

Adrianna knew she would be instantly drawn to somewhere different like Japan or China and definitely South America after Justine stories of adventure and misadventure. These locations would be fun, interesting and both so very different from their usual trip to the woodlands, town or visits to the city to see Rebecca and Fabio.

Jake then recounted his experience of Para-gliding in China and getting stuck by the Great Wall. Just as I started to think it was worth waiting three days for clear blue skies with a light breeze and low smog levels, for an aerial adventure that seemed like such a good idea at the time.

And it really was exciting and the views amazing, as I glided along just high enough to see crops of upland rice on the hillside and further on, folks tending to their rice paddies. I spotted a vineyard whose rows of vines seemed to extend forever over flat terrain. A tea plantation was also visible on hilly region that extended into the valley. The cotton plantation was easier to identify, due to the plant's white sprigs, as was the sugar plantations, with their tall bamboo stems and green foliage.

I was enjoying the aerial view of diverse terrain and architecture that defines the landscape. In the far distance, I could see a sprawling industrial zone, extensive road infrastructure and the skyscrapers of a super city that seemed to reach beyond the sky, and is home to bustling communities, powerful global corporations, medical centres, schools, universities, hotels and shopping malls.

Suddenly a strong gust of wind pushed me off course, and I found myself suspended on a ledge protruding from a cliff, almost hanging on by a thread, close to the side of a security watchtower on the Great Wall of China. An episode that triggered a major security alert with loud sounds of various alarms systems ringing and armed guards piling out of cars and trucks on the ground.

I tried desperately to activate my paraglide chute, and join others on the original path in the valley below. But at the same time, felt I was moments away from being shot at, as I didn't understand what was being said from the loudspeaker on the ground.

Finally, an official spoke in English, asking me to stay very still, stating how I was in a very dangerous situation - something I didn't need reminding of," said Jake.

At the same time, a helicopter sounded overhead and out popped two individuals in black fatigues who surrounded me on the cliff.

Seconds later, I was in the hangar, the safety and rescue equipment, removed and was seated beside an official in uniform. My armed clad military rescuers closely followed in quick succession, and the aircraft speed over the city and landed quickly. I was then driven to a police station and ushered quickly to an interview room by two guys, one in military uniform the other wearing a suit, who asked me to complete some documentation," recounted Jake.

"Shortly after, the doors behind me sung open and in walked the tour guide, accompanied by an official from the embassy." "Jake, there you are," said Herve. The guard checked the completed paperwork, asked me to sign it and said, "you are free to join your colleagues."

"With a sign of relief, I got up and went over to the others, and at this point felt like jelly with nerves. "But was lucky I didn't have to spend the night behind bars, as they just managed to catch the Ambassador, who was leaving for the airport. I felt extremely lucky to have been safely rescued, even though those guys were not amused, and I had no idea how it happened, or what the problem was," said Jake.

"Jake knowing you, there is always something," said Adrianna, "I know, but this was such a fluke accident. Another girl also landed off target too, but only a short distance from the planned position," said Jake.

"So make sure you don't unwittingly venture into unauthorized, off limits territory, otherwise you should be fine. And each location is unique, so everyone will find something special to remember.

I will never forget this particular adventure, apart from that time on safari in Kenya, when we almost got trod on by a giraffe and its young, who emerged from a wooded area, as we were taking pictures. Still it still paled into comparison to being almost shot at, for straying into a restricted security area by the Great Wall, and then rescued under reasonably tight security," said Jake.

"Not sure I will be so daring," said Adrianna. "Kenya sounds great too, so long as I don't let myself, Buddy or Perry get trod on by a Giraffe, while preoccupied with pictures," said Adrianna. I was thinking of maybe helping in a school or on a farm in Kenya. Meet some local folk and see first-hand how folk survive extended drought periods and soil erosion as result of global warming, and the farming methods being adapted to enhance crop yields.

"It's a perfect opportunity to explore the great outdoors of this vast continent too with a natural abundance of meadows, woodland, wetlands and wildlife makes for a real adventure," said Jake. "Only this time, Buddy and Perry would most likely be the hunted, not the hunters," said Jake. "And Perry the poodle would have no chance at all if something unusual caught his eye, as he would never see the danger," said Adrianna.

"If the great African outdoors became too daunting, then there is the world of art and architecture to savour, making this a strong possible location for part of the trip" said Adrianna." Absolutely right, as African art is really big news globally now, and the perfect souvenir," said Jake.

"From a seasonal perspective, America is perfect as we could go from the mountains to the beach in a couple of hours and enjoy the contrasting environments of prairielands, parklands, desert, woodlands, meadows and mountains as far as the eye can see and beyond. Tempting, very tempting," mulled Adrianna. "It's my kind of trip too," said Justine.

"I like the idea of exploring the great outdoors in a summer climate during our winter, so Australia and New Zealand are always exciting locations to enjoy nature and the natural environment.

"You are right," said Justine "and they are vast countries too especially if you have friends and relations located in different parts.

The selected location for a lifestyle and cultural break would crucially have to have employment opportunities too for the extended break.

It is the perfect time to get to the snow and Scandinavia would be just ideal. Maybe take a sleigh rides at the weekend, ski and visit Lapland. There is lots of space and freedom especially in this region, to explore the great outdoors with Perry the poodle and Buddy. Then travel onwards to Russia to see the art and architecture and the perfect place for a winter snow adventure. Justine then recounted her adventures in

Lapland a year earlier, as she and Frank stopped there whilst travelling though Scandinavia on the way back.

"I desperately wanted to take a sleigh ride from the town to the mountains," said Justine. The sleigh was pulled by about eight huskies. Everything was fine, in fact it was magical, as we breezed through the snow.

Soon the mountains came into view through the tall trees and we started to take pictures, when suddenly the sleigh stopped as a large tree branch fell across the path. The driver or musher, as he is known in Scandinavia, got out to clear the path and then made a call from his mobile phone. At the same time, the huskies started to move away and the sleigh started to gain speed. Next thing we were racing on down a huge slope, and all of a sudden were going off track through some tall trees, that towered into the sky above.

"We better try and stop them," said Frank, otherwise there is a risk of going over a cliff or crashing into one of the trees. Frank then shuffled to the front of the sleigh, but was unable to grab the reins, as it was trailing on the ground, while the huskies raced along.

I stood up but the sleigh went over a bump at the same time, and I was pushed down again," recounted Justine. "Oh my God Frank, what are we going to do and where are we now?"

The sleigh continued without a driver across a woodland path and out into a clearing, where the snow was lighter and slushier in places. "If I jump out, I still won't be able to catch or slow the huskies down," said Frank.

Suddenly, there was a huge bump, as the sleigh went over a ridge and sank down into a kind of hollow. The sleigh was now stuck or jammed in the hollow and the huskies were unable to move it on.

"Good and bad," said Justine, "well mostly good," said Frank "as God knows where we would end up, or for that matter where we were at that point," said Justine.

Frank then got out and could see that the sleigh was stuck in a hollow part of the ridge and he was unable to move it.

"Even if we could move or winch it free, not sure we could manage to steer the huskies and ourselves back to the original path, then find the driver or get some assistance," said Justine.

"Let's not panic yet," said Frank. "I think we had better try to get back on foot, and we may see or meet someone along the way who can call for assistance."

"We were in a total wilderness without a sound apart from the odd bird calling and the crunching of icy snow beneath our feet.

As we walked onwards, we saw reindeers grazing in the distance, on what little vegetation had emerged from under the permafrost. I suggested there were reindeer herders in these parts and we might meet some along the way," said Justine. I remembered reading a story sometime ago about 'The Reindeer People' who heard reindeer in cold snowy regions and move from place to place during the seasons.

According to the story, they are more likely to be in the valley in winter and early spring, and move further upland towards the mountains during the summer and autumn seasons, but Frank thought they lived further north in Siberia.

According to the guide book, local folk here also breed and herd reindeer as they produce milk, meat and hide and from time to time reindeer herds are culled to prevent over grazing of pasturelands," said Frank. Who suggested we may also see Rudolph, the elves and some Santa helpers along the way.

I suggested that we might even see some penguin, lemmings, wolverines or polar bears; as they mentioned this possibility at the welcome evening, saying how there is a variety of interesting wildlife in the area.

"Not sure I want to fight off a polar bear just at the moment and if the wolverines were any way peckish, they could instantly devourer a reindeer," said Frank drily.

"At this point, I was starting to get weary, as it's harder and more tiring trekking through the snow, but even though we were still stranded in Lapland, we were experiencing a truly beautiful winter wonderland, as the sun still glistened through the trees on to the frozen snow," recounted Justine.

"Just then a large eagle and some wild ducks flew from the spruce trees above, startling both of us as we trudged along, hoping for some sign of life, to get assistance or directions back to town. Still there were no sightings, apart the occasional calling of birds to disturb the silence as we walked through the snow that was frozen over in places.

We continued to follow the sleigh track back through the tall evergreen trees that according to our guidebook were Norwegian spruce, Scots pine and then further along some Larch and Birch trees. Soon we could see the mountains in the distance and even though we were on the original snow passage and going in the right direction, we were starting to get worried, as it would soon be dark," recounted Justine.

Suddenly we heard a loud crunching sound moving though the snow beyond the trees. It was an emergency snow mobile followed closely by two more vehicles.

Frank flagged down the startled duo and said, "Can you help us, we need to get back to the town." As we tried to explain, the two other snow mobiles ground to a halt behind. And out stepped Tryvke, our driver or sleigh Musher and greeted us, to our total relief," said Justin.

"Oh thank god," Frank said instantly, "we were trying to find our way back as the huskies and the sleigh got stuck in a hollow about two miles along through the tall trees at the bottom of a hill, and we were unable to free it," explained Frank. "Its fine," said Tryvke the sleigh musher, "we were coming out to find you, but it's more urgent now, as there is a weather warning in place for expected avalanches in this area. And because it is so close to the mountains, the danger levels have been raised. This means, all recreational activities including hunting, skiing and snowboarding will cease until further notice," explained Tryvke.

"The paramedics are here to help you guys and other folk who may need assistance. Patrols are also on stand-by with additional support, to ensure no one is stranded, as it will soon be dark.

"Gekkyi will drive you guys back now, and I will travel with the others to locate my sleigh and huskies," said the Musher. "Should we come with to help you," asked Frank – "Its better you guys get back now, as your guide and group are anxiously awaiting your return in the village, for dinner and after to enjoy an evening of music and song in view of the northern lights, which are spectacular this time of year. We will radio through now to say we have found you and you are on your way back," said Tryvke the Musher.

"And that was our stranded sleigh ride adventure in Lapland, which we laugh about now, but it wasn't so funny at the time. We did get some pictures great pictures, but it's still hard to explain the feeling of being lost in a magical wilderness, as it stirs many emotions, from anxiety to wonder and we discovered afterwards, we managed to cross over the border into Sweden," said Justine. "Sounds like a fun adventure," said Adrianna.

"I think Scandinavia is a really great location for a snow trip. As there is so much space to enjoy the great outdoors and makes for a pleasant adventure," said Adrianna. It is also close to Europe and central for onward travel east. Afterwards maybe move to a warmer Asian, Indian or Middle Eastern climate.

"It would be ideal to include two maybe three very different climates and cultures on the trip. The one thing I want to avoid in the chosen location is the monsoon season," said Adrianna. "That's wise, unless you have a specific itinerary or restricted options for time of travel," said Jake.

"I must get Rebecca on board too," said Adrianna. "You should," said Jake" and closer to the time I might decide to join you guys on this future adventure." "That would be fantastic and I think we would have a lot of fun too," said Adrianna.

"You guys would get a job no problem, and I could teach," said Justine. "They were always looking for native English language skills at the schools I worked in before," said Justine. "I think I'll be ok as I also have teacher training and work experience in this area. Great to catch up with you guys, it's almost like watching a movie, hearing of your global adventures," said Adrianna.

Ultimately, I will use my own guidelines to establish the suitability of a location, thought Adrianna.

I would still like to be reasonably close to friendly and unfriendly neighbours in the surrounding area. The woodland and wildlife will be very different, and I'll need to be aware of the dangerous or hostile species that could unexpectedly appear.

Therefore, safety will apply at all times when selecting a suitable location for adventure in the surrounding woodlands and meadows. And hopefully there will be a lake close by, to have a picnic, sail, and fish or feed the ducks.

Last, but not least, opportunities for work will be important and we may even meet some Reggie the robot types in action along the way. Folks are paid more to manage Robots at work in these countries than do the actual job themselves. Finding a suitable teaching role would be just ideal, thought Adrianna, and time permitting, maybe help voluntarily on a conservation project also.

Schools, Universities, cultural centres, museums, galleries, exhibitions and lectures in the neighbourhood or close by would make destination almost perfect, thought Adrianna.

Then it will just be a question of organising the holiday plans and journey details with a map and checklist. Not forgetting the additional medical and visa applications issues.

Trip essentials would include clothes, shoes or boots and accessories to pack, which will depend on the location and local weather conditions. And finally, my reconnaissance fact-finding diary, to note key points of reference on each place of interest visited for the one time or sometime cultural and lifestyle experience abroad.

I know Rebecca, Fabio, Justine and Jake may like to come along or offer advice and guidance closer to the time. Even recount further stories from their adventures, discoveries and dreams while exploring faraway lands.

14

THE DREAM

Adrianna rang Jake to tell him about how she dreamt that she went parachuting with Buddy and Perry the poodle over the Amazon rainforest. Recounting how for this particular trip they had to have low visibility balloon and clothing that also blended in and suited a jungle environment so as not to startle the inhabitants and wildlife species of the rainforest. The hot air balloon was in the shape of a large green Frog with huge eyes.

Buddy had a mini-dragon costume the same colour, and Perry the poodle had a peacock type costume, so to balance his weight as evenly as possible.

Buddy and Perry looked really funny in their dragon and peacock costumes with goggles and safety headgear. We tried to land on a grassy area close to rocks but got suspended in some trees. Nevertheless, it felt safe as we had a good view of the forest from every direction and could just focus on getting the balloon free," recounted Adrianna.

"Suddenly Perry somehow triggered the emergency chute, which propelled us into the air, while he yelped loudly. Buddy panicked and I tried to stay calm, as we gained altitude, and was just high enough to get the balloon free but still hovering over tall tropical trees below.

Buddy and Perry were now yelping and barking loudly, which echoed far into the sky and deep into the forest. Both were starting to get breathless and sounding hoarse with fear and panic as they bounced back and forth in the carriage of the balloon.

The balloon was suddenly dropping again rapidly towards the trees luckily near the underlying grassy area beneath, in a space created by loggers who cut down trees to create pastureland for their herds of cattle. It was a rare and lucky opening in the dense canopy of trees, that covered the entire rainforest.

We were all panicked at this point and both puppies were still yelping loudly, especially if a weird bird came into view, as we continued to float above the pericarp and mahogany trees. The balloon was almost fully inflated again, and I think because we were so close to the ground, it looked huge.

The puppies continued to yelp loudly and I was nervous too as we floated around for about almost 45 minutes, unable to get the balloon to land safely and away from the trees. Buddy was trembling at this point and then went limp, but Perry continued yelping and was getting breathless and hoarse at the same time.

We eventually landed close to a circle of large Banana trees or similar. Two huge eagles or maybe falcons flew from the overhead trees and a flock of very colourful birds, like the macaws or toucans maybe, called out loudly and flew from the nearby trees,

" I tried to untangle the balloon and deflate it, while Buddy and Perry now somewhat recovered from their in flight ordeal, sniffed around.

I then heard a loud pounding or thudding sound that echoed further in the distance, deep in the forest, with various screeching and buzzing sounds, from what appeared to be all forms of forest inhabitants on the move.

"I then managed to drag the balloon towards the rocks on higher ground, to make it easier for the helicopter to spot us," said Adrianna.

What at this point sounded like a stampede, seemed to get louder and more urgent, as everything seemed to be moving or racing to a new grazing, or resting area.

If you consider the rainforest is home to some hundreds of mammals including dangerous species like cougars and jaguars, not counting the many spices of birds from eagles to ostriches of every imaginable colour, size and shape, along with the hundreds of other species from the reptile and amphibian families, you can just imagine the scene.

It was starting to get cold and I was nervous at the thought of having to spend the night in the rainforest, as there was still no news or response from base, and I was starting to get very worried.

Luckily, I had some light snacks and shared them with Perry and Buddy who had just recovered," recounted Adrianna. "My Para-gliding adventure by the Great Wall of China was not nearly as exciting as your dream - what did you do then," asked Jake.

"I sent two flares into the evening sky that I hoped would guide the rescue helicopter to our location in the tropical rain forest.

A short while later could hear loud pounding of drums and from our position on the rocks, see smoke emitting from fires lit in different areas.

Suddenly, I noticed tribal natives moving quickly through the trees below, and more followed, as if on some urgent mission.

We then waited one maybe two hours, with no sign of our rescue helicopter to take us back. Evening was starting to close in and fear starting to grip, as it would soon be dark, when suddenly there was a flickering movement in the faraway distance that got louder as it moved closer. I hoped it was our rescue helicopter, but was still nervous they might not spot us and then relieved as the red helicopter started to round down close to where we waited," said Adrianna.

"The helicopter finally landed in a savannah area further down to our left, which was a huge relief, as I thought we would have to spend the night in the darkness of the tropical rainforest with unknown danger lurking in the background.

I then took Buddy and Perry down to the waiting helicopter and was met by two rangers, who almost accused me of trespassing," said Adrianna.

"The forest Rangers said they had reports of evil spirits and devils in the forest, and the native tribes were spooked.

I explained how we were spooked too, as you can imagine, watching what looked like a kind of stampede just inches below us," explained Adrianna.

"There were complications with the landing gear on the balloon and we were hovering or floating above the dense forest canopy for about forty-five minutes trying to land, and after waited and watched the stamped. I also caught a glimpse of some tribal natives who seemed oblivious to our presence at that point, as they hurried along to wherever," explained Adrianna.

"Well lady, they were spooked, very spooked, as you posed a different threat they had never witnessed before, because you weren't the usual loggers or herders clearing tracks of the rainforest to gain increased land ownership and additional grazing pastures for their cattle herds. Even though such practices are now illegal, due to the impact of global warming," explained the Ranger.

"And you weren't miners drilling for gold or working on the dam building project, which they wholly oppose for the most part, but at least would be familiar with such construction activity and the various government representatives coming and going to these parts to negotiate, advise and work on the dam building project. So without a doubt, the native tribes imagined a sign or warning from the gods or spirits of doom.

You must remember too, the tribes are hunters and gathers – this is their life and lifeline. A hunting and gathering tradition, which has remained unchanged and hidden from the outside world for hundreds of years, in fact, some tribes have never been seen by anyone from the western world. Then suddenly their hunting ground is empty, devoid of all animals which were now running scared, their plants and harvest trod on, trees and fruits damaged and the list goes on.

Their immediate view was their Gods were angry and wanted to punish them by taking their food and destroying their livelihoods. And don't forget it is also close to harvest time, when they are particularly sensitive to the Gods and honour them through various rituals. You guys threw their world into instant disarray, which is why you probably caught a glimpse of them moving urgently," said the Ranger.

"We saw your flare but were awaiting instructions from an earlier message to say your guide and helicopter developed a technical fault that needed immediate repair.

You are lucky as you were easier to spot due to your position at the emergent level of the rain forest, which is at higher altitude or at the top of the tall trees. Had you been suspended underneath the canopy, you would have been harder to spot and rescue, especially if we got to nightfall. And if you were stranded or stuck at the understory or forest floor level of the tropical rain forest, it would have taken longer as we would have to wait for the stamped to end, before travelling on foot to rescue you.

We were on standby for emergencies and saw the flares in the meantime, but you are somewhat off course – you should have landed south to southwest of this point," said the Ranger, who finally introduced himself as Bob and his co-pilot colleague as Rodrigos.

"We were also on the lookout for illegal loggers too, as we thought originally they were responsible for events."

"Maybe they also contributed to the stampede," said Adrianna. "Oh no lady, rarely have I seen this type of disturbance in the forest," said Bob the Forest Ranger. "And you are saying this is our fault, but you must understand there was nothing we could do," said Adrianna – "as our balloon got stuck. And Perry and Buddy panicked when suspended mid-air and if that wasn't traumatic enough, we were left with the possibility of being stranded for the night," pleaded Adrianna. "At that stage my dream ended Jake, I was starting to wake up feeling exhausted, confused, and not sure if I was stranded in mid air or in the tropical rainforest," said Adrianna

"No wonder, what a dream, my adventures sound boring in comparison," said Jake. "Not at all," replied Adrianna, "because you and Justine lived the dream, that's the difference. I remembered your story threads as I tried to put some ideas together for a similar adventure," said Adrianna.

"My dream was like seeing a movie or being there, as it seemed so real," said Adrianna. "I believe you," said Jake. "The planning stage really is the most difficult part, as there is so much to organise, but it's also very exciting," said Jake.

"Absolutely, so I just need to make a list of things to do, plan the trip outline with journey details, pack luggage with travel essentials, to make a world of adventure, discovery and dreams all come true," said Adrianna.

The End

STORY REFERENCE POINTS

River Rhine -
Interesting historic and present-day facts;

Location and Path

One of Europe's longest rivers and most important inland waterways starts as a stream from source as source from a glacier high above sea level in the Swiss Alps.

The Rhine forms the border with Austria, Principality of Lichtenstein, Germany and France as it continues north into the Netherlands flowing into the North Sea at Rotterdam.

The Rhine assumes three different names depending on the country it flows through. In Germany it is called the Rhein, in France it is called the Rhine and in the Netherlands it is called the Rijn.

The Rhine River and its many tributaries provide drinking water for large parts of southern Germany.

A key transportation route through Europe over the centuries as goods and raw materials are transported on its waterway since Roman Empire times.

The river assumes different shapes as it progresses through Europe.

Widening at a point in Switzerland, narrowing through the Rhine Gorge and at other points, as it flows through Germany, where the landscape changes to form a steep sided valley, filled with vineyards and castles overlooking the river.

Definition: A Glacier: is a slow moving-mass of ice and snow, formed by snow falling and accumulating over the years, descending down a steep mountain (Alpine glacier) as in a valley glacier or extending from a central mass as in a Continental glacier.

GLOBAL TIME ZONES

Global Time Zones from Dublin or London

When its 12 noon in Dublin or London its:

- **8am** in Venezuela, South America - **4** hours (Venezuela is 4hrs behind Dublin or London)

- **3pm** in Riyadh, Saudi Arabia **+ 3** hours (Riyadh is 3hrs ahead of Dublin or London)

- **8pm** in Singapore **+ 8** hours (Singapore is 8hrs ahead of Dublin or London)

- **9pm** in Tokyo, Japan **+ 9** hours

- **7am** in New York, USA **– 5** hours

- **2pm** in Cairo, Egypt **+ 2** hours

- **4am** in Palo Alto, USA **– 8** Hours

- **1pm** in Brussels, Belgium, **+1**

IDEAS AND ACTIVITY SPACE

SAFETY REFERENCE POINTS

Road Safety/Safe Cross Code

- Look for a safe place to cross
- Don't hurry, stop and wait.
- Let all the traffic pass.
- Look around, listen and look again before you cross the road.
- When the road is clear, walk straight across, looking all around at the same time until you reach the other side safely.
- At traffic lights, wait until the light is green and all the traffic has stopped, before crossing.
- Remember to wear your high visibility vest when walking on public roads.

Water Safety Code and points to remember

- When outdoors at the lake or the beach, consider the general conditions of the water as it may be very cold or there may be hidden currents.
- It can be difficult to get out of the water.
- The water can be deep, even deeper than you realise or difficult to estimate the depth.
- There may be no lifeguards to advise you or provide assistance if you get into difficulty.
- There may be hidden rubbish such as broken glass or the water may be polluted.

Safe Cycling Code and points to note

- Look behind before you overtake or stop.
- Use Arm Signals before turning right or left.
- Obey traffic lights and road signs.
- Don't ride on the pavement unless there is a sign saying you can.
- On busy or narrow roads, do not cycle next to another person, cycle behind or before them.
- Do not listen to music, or use your mobile phone when cycling.
- When overtaking parked cars, watch out for doors opening suddenly.
- Always wear you cycle helmet and reflective high visibility vest/clothing.

Pony trekking safety

- Ensure you are comfortable and know the pony or horse before taking out on a busy road.
- Always wear your riding hat
- Wear a high visibility vest

OTHER KEY POINTS OF INTEREST

Vineyard: Vines grow in the vineyard and grapes are the fruit of the vine.

Activity: The grapes are harvested to make wine and other drinks.

Produce: Varieties of wines, Champaign and related spirits

Location: France, Germany, Spain, Switzerland (has the highest vineyard in Europe). Many countries globally with suitable soil and climatic conditions also have vineyards. China has the largest wine producing area in the world, followed by Spain and France is 3rd largest producer of wine. The USA and UK are the largest importers of wines.

Harvesting: Is the picking of the grapes and a first step in wine production. Grapes are either harvested mechanically or by hand. After the harvest, grapes are taken into a winery and prepared for ferment.

Production: White wine is made from pressing the crushed grapes to extract the juice, after the first stage in fermentation the skin removed and has no other purpose. Whereas Red wine is made from the pulp of red and black grapes and fermentation occurs with the grape skins, this gives the wine its dark red colour.

Vineyards in France:
Loire Valley
Bordeaux
Alsace
Visperterminen, Switzerland (Europe's highest vineyard)

AMAZON RAINFOREST –
INTERESTING FACTS AND FIGURES

Amazon Rainforest is the largest tropical rainforest in the world.

Location: South America and extends over eight countries in South America. They are Brazil, Bolivia, Peru, Ecuador, Colombia, Venezuela, Guyana and Suriname.

The Amazon River flows through the rainforest giving it its name.

The Amazon River is the second longest river in the world after the Nile.

A tropical rainforest is defined in terms of location from the Equator.

A variety of landscape types are found in the Amazon rainforest and include Rainforests, Floodplains, Savannahs, Swamplands and Rivers.

The Amazon is situated 28 degrees north of the Equator.

There are four layers or levels in the tropical rain forest as follows.
Ground level or forest floor is very dark with few plants and decomposing leaves and waste material from the overhead layers. Various insect species help to decompose the waste material and it is then absorbed by the roots of the trees.

Understory level reaches from about to about 12 feet or 3.5 meters. The understory level receives less light than the layers above it. However, it is still frequented by many different types of animals, particularly insects.

Canopy level consists of a layer of trees that are between75 to 120 feet in height. 90% of rainforest life is found here because the air is very humid and many plants are able to grow on the trees, like vines, mosses and, lichens.

The Emergent level is the highest layer of the tropical rainforest and receives greatest amount of light. Trees grow to between 120 – 250 feet in height, and characteristically have umbrella shaped tops, few branches and huge trunks.

The Amazon rainforest is home to 600 types of Animal including many dangerous species.

2 and a half million Insect species inhabit the Amazon Rainforest

20% of the world bird species live in the Amazon forest.

There are 40000 different Trees /Plants and plant species in the Amazon rainforest.

A vast array of commodities are produced in the Amazon like livestock, leather, soy, oil, gas and minerals. These are exported to China, Russia, the USA and other countries.

The Rainforest used to cover 14% of Earth's surface, but due to deforestation i.e. logging, it now only covers 6%
17% of the Forest cover has been lost in the last 50 years

More than 25% of natural medicines have been found in the rainforest
Over two hundred plant species are used for food and medicinal purposes
The most popular medicinal plant is the Pau d'Acro used to treat a number of ailments from cancer to allergies.

Modern day threats to the rainforest.

Tree logging and deforestation – the Amazon forest has lost lots of tree increasing the impact of global warming.
Mining for gold damages the Amazon habitat as the methods used poison and pollutes the water and soil and destroys fertile land.

The Amazon is home to more than 350 different ethnic groups.

According to recent studies, an increase in temperatures of 3 degrees would destroy about 75% of the Amazon.

THE OCEAN —

INTERESTING FACTS AND FIGURES

70% of Earth's surface is covered by ocean

Average Ocean temperature is 3.9 degrees Celsius and 39 degrees Fahrenheit, but ranges to below freezing in the Arctic to 37 degrees Celsius or 98 degrees Fahrenheit in the Arabian Gulf.

The ocean supports all living organisms: fish in the sea, birds in the sky, and animals and humans on land. It regulates climates and our weather, including tsunamis, the killer waves caused by earthquakes on the ocean floor and undersea volcanic eruptions.

We use products derived from sea life every day, ranging from kelp in shampoo to algae in ice cream and seaweed in toothpaste and peanut butter.

Marine plants provide most of the oxygen that we breathe, and fish and wild seafood are viable options to eradicate famine, if we protect and sustainably manage our ocean and its ecosystems. That's a staggering figure, considering we catch more than 80 million tonnes of fish annually.

As a collective population, humans are throwing an equivalent of one garbage truck of waste—including plastic bags and soda bottles—into the ocean every minute, posing serious threats to marine life and human health and safety.

A report from 2016 warns that there will be more plastic in the ocean than fish by 2050—unless we clean up our act. The estimate for the amount of plastic in the ocean by mid-century is a whopping 950 million tonnes.

More than 90 percent of international trade is conducted over the seas. Maritime shipping is essential to the world's economy, with the ocean serving as a super-highway for global trade and communications.

Using ships for trading between countries is the most cost-effective means of moving goods across the Earth. Shipping traffic is also one of the human activities that has an adverse impact on the ocean's biodiversity and marine life.

Earth has various land masses, but there is just one big global ocean. This vast body of water is geographically divided into five distinctly named bodies, with their boundaries evolving over time: the Pacific Ocean, Atlantic Ocean, Indian Ocean, Arctic Ocean, and Southern Ocean (or Antarctic Ocean).

The Pacific Ocean is the largest and deepest of the Earth's oceanic divisions.

The Earth's "tallest mountain" is Mauna Kea (not Everest!), but more than half lies beneath the ocean.

A dormant volcano in Hawaii, Mauna Kea measures 10,210 metres (or 33,500 feet) from its watery base on the Pacific floor to its summit. Compare that to Mount Everest's 8,848 metres (29,029 feet) above sea level.

The world's longest mountain range is also underwater. Stretching an impressive 65,000 kilometres (40,390 miles) long, the Mid-Oceanic Ridge is an extensive chain of mountains running across the Atlantic and into the Pacific and Indian oceans. It accounts for nearly 25 percent of the Earth's total surface!

The ocean is a living, breathing (and the world's largest) museum.

Home to more than one million known species of animals and plants, scientists say there may be as many as two million species that remain a complete mystery. And let's not forget about the artefacts from shipwrecks over centuries!

Oceans make up 99 percent of the Earth's habitable space.

Which means it's the largest space in our universe known to be inhabited by living organisms. The world's largest biological structure is found in the ocean: Australia's.

94 percent of life on Earth is aquatic.

Oceans contain 97 percent of the Earth's water supply.

Two to three percent is contained in glaciers and ice caps. Less than one percent of this supply is fresh water. In fact, if the ocean's total salt content were dried, it would cover all the Earth's land to a depth of five feet.

Three times as much garbage is dumped into the ocean as the weight of fish caught every year.

The ocean has lakes and rivers.

Salt in seawater dissolves to form depressions in the ocean floor. It also makes the water in the area denser, so that it settles into the depressions. These underwater lakes and rivers (also referred to as brine pools) have shorelines, and even waves, like their land counterparts.

The ocean also has waterfalls. The Earth's largest waterfall is located underwater between Greenland and Iceland. The Denmark Strait cataract (or Greenland Pump) drops an astounding 3,505 metres (11,500 feet), three times the height of Angel Falls in Venezuela.

Six million cubic feet of water goes over Niagara Falls every minute. The Denmark Strait cataract carries 175 million cubic feet of water per second. That's equal to 2,000 Niagaras at peak flow.

NATURE TRAIL ACTIVITIES, IDEAS AND PROJECTS

Identify type, age, period in history and origin of four trees.

Identify three types of birds, their sounds, and nesting patterns.

Observations: Other forms of wild life and their movement/ trail and habitat e.g.; fox, badger, hedgehog, rabbit or hare.

Note the variations in woodland and marshland vegetation.

Identify three types of spring posies or flora and note with a short description.

Discuss the impact of pollution and global warming on the natural environment. And the useful role played by deciduous trees.

Imagine how different your own natural environment is likely to be from a nature trail in Africa's Kenya. Research the different type of trees, plants and animals you are likely to encounter in the woodlands, parklands, wetlands and deserts on this other continent.

Art Project: Draw and paint a scene from a nature trail, or select your season of choice, for a woodland and wildlife picture.

Project: Design a seasonal school nature table or a wall collage.

A WORLD OF ADVENTURE DISCOVERY AND DREAMS now goes off the page, offline and off track. Because now you know... you've read the book ... don't wait for the movie. Take action now and make your adventure of discovery and dreams really happen.

SO FORGET TECHNOLOGY FOR A DAY ... and go see, go do, go plan the adventure ... go beyond and enjoy the trip.

SPRING/SUMMER/AUTUMN ACTIVITY
Enjoy the Great Outdoors

Appreciate nature and diverse natural environments
Bike or Hike, Climb, Walk, Pony trek, or Run in the;
Woodlands
Meadows
Marsh, Ferns and Bog lands
Mountains
Swim, Surf, Sail, Kayak, Fish or Snorkel in the;
Ocean, Lakes, Rivers,
Have a picnic or Barbecue at the Beach

ALL SEASONS ACTIVITY
Things to do... take a class and see how to make or create something new
Draw a picture, take a picture, colour a picture or make a picture
Design some cards
Design some clothing, knitwear
Design and build a tree house, a little house and furniture

Make the cake, the cookies, the juice, lemonade, smoothes, jelly, jam, relish and wine.

Go to the movies or make a movie

Discover Heritage, History, Geography and Archaeology of the natural environment:
Visit a Castle, Historic Monument or Museum
Explore an Archaeology trail
Walk the way of the pilgrims

Plan, prepare, party - put it all together with the movie, the wine, some cookies, cakes, pizza offerings and ice cream.

Dream your dream and make it happen!

IDEAS AND ACTIVITY SPACE

ABOUT THE AUTHOR

A Business Graduate and English language Tutor.

I was inspired to create this story series partly because of my love of nature and contrasting natural environments that transcend time, passing trends, and links cultures across international boundaries, in a constantly changing world, where nature and the natural environment is a constant and permanent force.

BIBLIOGRAPHY

Global landscapes

The Dorling Kindersley Science Encyclopaedia

The Atlas of the Environment, by Geoffrey Lean and Don Hinrichsen

Earth – the Definitive Visual guide, by James F. Luhr and Jeffrey E. Post

Earth Inc. By Al Gore

Understanding Earth, by Thomas Jordan, John Grafzinger, Raymond Sieve

The Ocean, Our Future – A report of the Independent World Commission on the Ocean
Edited by, Peter Coates, David Moon, P. Warde

The Rainforest – A Panoramic Vision, by Patrick Hook, Chartwell Press

Local landscapes

Exploring the History and Heritage of Irish Landscapes, by Patrick J. Duffy

Tohar Phadraig, by Balintubber Abbey Publications

Irish Wildlife, Birds, Animals and Plants, by Gordon D'Arcy

Wild Mayo, by Michael Viney

Ancient Ireland from Pre-History to Middle-Ages, by Jacqueline O'Brien and Peter Harbison

A Beginners Guide to Ireland's Seashore, A Sherkin Island Marine Station Publication